台科大圖書
since 1997

高中 English conversation
英文會話 素養
Easy Go!

許雅惠 編著

影音教學說明：
為方便讀者學習，本書教學影音請至本公司MOSME行動學習一點通網站（https://mosme.net/），於首頁的搜尋欄輸入本書關鍵字（例如：書號、書名、作者）進行搜尋，尋得該書後於「學習資源」頁籤點選「影音教學」各單元之「影音開啟」觀看影片。

序言

想開口說英文,卻沒什麼英文基礎,只會英文入門題卜單字,或者單字量只有 500～800 字的初學者,在面對外國人與接受英文基本口說檢定時,該怎麼辦呢?

本書集結了日常生活常用的 15 個主題,從點餐到描述過去經驗、不同情境下自己的作法,還有對於人事物的形容等,並按照題卜書系列書籍編排精神,由簡入深、循序漸進,將相似的答題技巧放在一起,讓讀者可以舉一反三,說出一口好英文!

讀完本書,在面對任何英檢口說、升學考試,甚至出國前的基本英文檢定時,一定都能輕鬆過關,從此不再害怕開口說英文。

在此要特別感謝台科大圖書范總經理的肯定與允諾,才能順利出版本書,希望本書的出版能幫助到莘莘學子學好基礎英文會話,也可搭配題卜書系列的其他叢書進行學習,必定能相得益彰,讓英文成為自己的一大利器!

許雅惠　謹致

目錄

Unit 1
Weather and favorite time of day 1
天氣 / 最愛時光

Unit 2
Places and adjectives 10
地點與形容詞

Unit 3
Who / Wearing / Personality 22
誰 / 穿著 / 形容個性、習性、天分

Unit 4
When / How long? / How much? 36
何時 / 多久？ / 多少？

Unit 5
Frequency 48
頻率

Unit 6
What to eat? 56
吃什麼？

Unit 7
How to do it? / Methods 64
如何做？ / 方法

Unit 8
What do you do in your leisure time? — 72
你在閒暇時做些什麼？

Unit 9
Likes and favorites — 90
喜歡與最愛

Unit 10
Make an order — 102
點餐

Unit 11
Make a phone call — 114
電話用語

Unit 12
Opinions and views — 124
描述己見與敘述看法

Unit 13
Love or money? Happy or sad? — 134
二選一

Unit 14
Past experience — 144
過去經驗

Unit 15
What will you do in these situations? — 152
在…的狀況下，你會怎麼做？

一起來看看幕後花絮吧！

Unit 1

請至 MOSME 觀看教學影片

Weather and favorite time of day
天氣 / 最愛時光

❓ Core questions :

Q1. What's the weather going to be like tomorrow?
Q2. How is the weather in Taiwan?
　　Describe the weather in Taiwan.
Q3. Which season do you like best? Why?
Q4. What is your favorite time of day? Why?

要和人聊得開心，總是需要一個話題做開頭，而天氣或季節，就是一個很好的話題喔！趕快來學天氣相關的英文單字與句子吧～

GO! GO! GO!

Ms.Tips & Ponyo's daily conversation

How is the weather in Taiwan?

It is warm in spring,

hot in summer,

cool in autumn,

…and cold in winter.

Words to use

1 Feeling 冷熱感受

| warm 溫暖 | | dry 乾燥 | cool 涼爽 | fresh 清新 | bracing 清爽微冷 |

| cold 冷 | chilly 寒冷 | freezing cold 凍寒 | frosty 冷到結霜 | |

| cozy 舒適宜人 | hot 熱 | humid 濕熱 | | moist / damp 潮濕 |

| boiling hot 炎熱 | burning hot 炙熱 | scorching hot 酷熱 | |

2 Weather 天氣

| sunny 晴天 | clear 晴朗 | breezy 微風 | windy 多風的 | stormy 暴風 |

| foggy 多霧的 | misty 濃霧的 | cloudy 陰天 | hailing 冰雹的 | | drizzly 小雨的 |

| rainy 下雨的 | showery 陣雨的 | snowy 下雪的 | thundery 有雷的 | |

3 Season 季節

spring	summer	fall / autumn	winter
春	夏	秋	冬

4 Time of day 一日時光

early morning	sunrise / dawn		morning
清晨	日出、晨曦		早上

noon		afternoon	sunset / dusk
中午		下午	日落、黃昏

after school	evening	night	
放學後	晚上	夜晚	

認識完關於天氣與季節的單字後，先來暖身練習吧！請試著依圖片情境寫出以天氣為主題的對話。

How to answer the question

Q1. What's the weather going to be like tomorrow?

> 註：注意問答句的時態為「未來式」。

Ans.1 It *is going to* be rainy and windy tomorrow because a typhoon is coming. I think I should take an umbrella or a raincoat with me. Besides, I will take a bus to school instead of riding a bike. It will be safer to take a public transportation in such a windy day.

Ans.2 It *is going to* be sunny tomorrow. In spring and summer, the weather is usually sunny and hot. I like sunny days because I can do a lot of outdoor activities, such as basketball, baseball and soccer. They are my favorite sports. I can play sports with my friends after school on such sunny days.

✏️ **It's your turn! Write your answer down below:**

_____
_____
_____
_____
_____
_____
_____

Q2. How is the weather in Taiwan?
Describe the weather in Taiwan.

Ans.1 It is warm in spring, hot in summer, cool in autumn and cold in winter. In my opinion, I like spring best. It is not too hot and not too cold. Trees and flowers bloom in spring, and the weather is pleasing. It is a wonderful time for going camping and hiking.

Ans.2 It is warm in spring, hot in summer, cool in autumn and cold in winter. In my opinion, I like summer best because I enjoy sunshine very much. I can go swimming in sunny days. Once in a while, I can go surfing and then take the sunbath at the beach.

✏️ **It's your turn! Write your answer down below:**

Q3. Which season do you like best? Why?

Ans.1 In my opinion, I like autumn/ fall best. It is not too hot or too cold. I can go mountain climbing with my family members and enjoy the breeze along the mountain path. It is the most pleasing season in Taiwan.

In my opinion,... 依我之見	As for me ... 至於我…
= From my point of view, ...	As for me , I'm going home.
= As far as I am concerned, ...	至於我，我要回家。

Ans.2 From my point of view, I like winter best. I prefer cold and dry weather to hot and humid days. I can go skiing in South Korea or in Japan. I like to go jogging in the early morning and enjoy the cold air blowing on my face, which refresh my body and mind.

✏️ **It's your turn! Write your answer down below:**

_____
_____
_____
_____
_____
_____
_____

Q4. What is your favorite time of a day? Why?

Ans.1 From my point of view, I like morning best. It is in the morning that I feel most energetic. After a night of good sleep, I restore my energy and refresh my mind. I can see things clearly and do things best in the morning. That's the reasons why I like morning best.

> 註：強調句型 It is...that...。

Ans.2 As far as I am concerned, I like evening. The class is over and I can go back to my sweet home. I can take my time watching TV and eating dinner with my family instead of being so busy following a tight school schedule. I can also play mobile games or chat with friends online. I feel comfortable and relaxed in the evening. That's why I think evening is the best time of a day.

✏ It's your turn! Write your answer down below:

_____
_____
_____
_____
_____
_____
_____

Unit 2

請至 MOSME 觀看教學影片

Places and adjectives
地點與形容詞

? Core questions :

Q1. Where did you go last weekend?

Q2. Where were you born?
What's your hometown like?
Describe your hometown.

Q3. Where do you usually go when you eat out?

Q4. Have you ever been to other countries? If not, which country would you like to go? Why?
What is your favorite country? And why?

Q5. Describe your living room at home.

週末時去了哪裡？通常都吃什麼呢？只要學會本章內容就能流暢地與朋友聊聊去過的國家甚至是家裡的擺設喔！

Let's get started!

Unit 2 Places and adjectives | 11

Ms.Tips & Ponyo's daily conversation

Words to use

1 Region 地區

| big city 大城 | small town 小鎮 | village 村莊 | tourist attraction 觀光勝地 |

| in the mountains 山區 | at the seaside 海邊 |

northern/central/southern/eastern Taiwan
北 / 中 / 南 / 東台灣

2 Characteristic 特色

traditional snacks
傳統小吃

famous product/specialty
名產

convenient public transportation
便利的公共運輸

wonderful weather
美好天氣

comfortable climate
氣候宜人

splendid scenery
壯麗景色

peaceful landscape
寧靜景色

beautiful scenery
美景

picturesque landscape
如畫般的景色

Unit 2 Places and adjectives 13

3 Location 地點

| fancy restaurant 高級餐廳 | seafood restaurant 海鮮餐廳 | fast-food restaurant 速食店 |

| Japanese-food restaurant 日式餐廳 |  hot-pot restaurant 火鍋店 |

|  steak house 排餐廳 | cafeteria 自助餐 |

| café 簡餐店 | noodle stand 小麵攤 | night market 夜市 |

請參考漫畫內容並利用以上單字，試著寫出一小段關於地點與形容的對話吧！

How to answer the question

Q1. Where did you go last weekend?

> 註：注意答句的時態為「過去式」。

Ans.1 I went to visit my grandparents with my family last weekend. My grandparents live in Tainan, which is located in southern Taiwan. Tainan is famous for its traditional snacks. We especially like to eat stinky tofu, which is delicious and yummy.

Ans.2 I went to Kenting, which is located in the southern part of Taiwan. Kenting is famous for its wonderful weather and natural beauty. I also went hiking in Kenting National Park and went to the sea for snorkeling.

✏ It's your turn! Write your answer down below:

Q2. Where were you born?
What's your hometown like?
Describe your hometown.

Ans.1 I was born in Taipei, which is located in northern Taiwan. Taipei is the biggest city in Taiwan and is famous for its convenient public transportation. People can take the MRT or buses to go to school or work.

Ans.2 Taitung is my hometown. It is located in eastern Taiwan. Taitung is famous for its hot springs, especially Jhihben* hot springs and picturesque landscape. I was born in a peaceful village, Chishang* and its rice production, such as meal box, is popular all over the island.

*Jhihben 知本
*Chishang 池上

✏️ **It's your turn! Write your answer down below:**

Q3. Where do you usually go when you eat out?

Ans.1 I usually go to McDonald's with my friends. We like fast food, such as fried chicken, French fries, and Cola. Eating too much of them is not good for our health. However, they are so yummy and tasty that we love them very much.

Ans.2 I usually go to a seafood restaurant. There are several seafood restaurants near my house because I live in a fish village near the ocean. While my parents are busy with work, they usually take me to one of the seafood restaurants to enjoy our dinner. Seafood, such as crabs, oyster omelet*, fish, shrimps, etc, is delicious but not very expensive. We often have a good time enjoying our dinner there.

*oyster omelet 蚵仔煎

Unit 2 Places and adjectives | 17

Ans.3 I usually go to a nearby noodle stand with my family. I like to eat noodles, especially beef noodles. They are delicious but cheap. We usually order several bowls of noodles and some vegetables for dinner.

✏️ **It's your turn! Write your answer down below:**

_____
_____
_____
_____
_____
_____
_____

Q4. Have you ever **been to** other countries?
If not, which country would you like to go? Why?
What is your favorite country? And Why?

> 註：注意答句的時態為「現在完成式」。

Ans.1 No, I have not been to any other country. If I could, I would like to go to Japan. It is famous for the architecture of many old temples. In addition, its people have the reputation* of being very polite and honest. By the way, I like traditional Japanese clothes because they are graceful and elegant.

*reputation 聲譽

Ans.2 No, I have not been to any other country. If I could, I would like to go to South Korea. The country is famous for its K-music and soap operas. Many features in movies and soap operas conducted by South Korea become internationally famous movie stars, including my idol. I also like its traditional food, pickles, which it is spicy, but wonderful.

Ans.3 No, I have not been to any other country. If I could, I would like to go to Australia. There are many famous animals in Australia, such as koalas and kangaroos. They are unique to Australia and can't be found anywhere else. By the way, they are so cute and interesting. I cannot wait to have a trip to this country.

✏️ **It's your turn! Write your answer down below:**

Q5. Describe your living room at home.

Ans.1 My living room is big, but usually in a mess. There are toys, clothes, socks, books all over my living room. My younger sister is nine years old, and she never cleans the living room. I usually clean it once a week, but it will be messy before long.

Ans.2 My living room is little, but cozy*, clean and tidy. Everything is in its position, so I can easily fetch something if I need it. There are a TV, a sofa and three bookshelves in my living room. It is also equipped with an air-conditioner. Therefore, I can enjoy a wonderful atmosphere with a pleasant temperature even in hot summer days.

*cozy 愜意

✏ It's your turn! Write your answer down below:

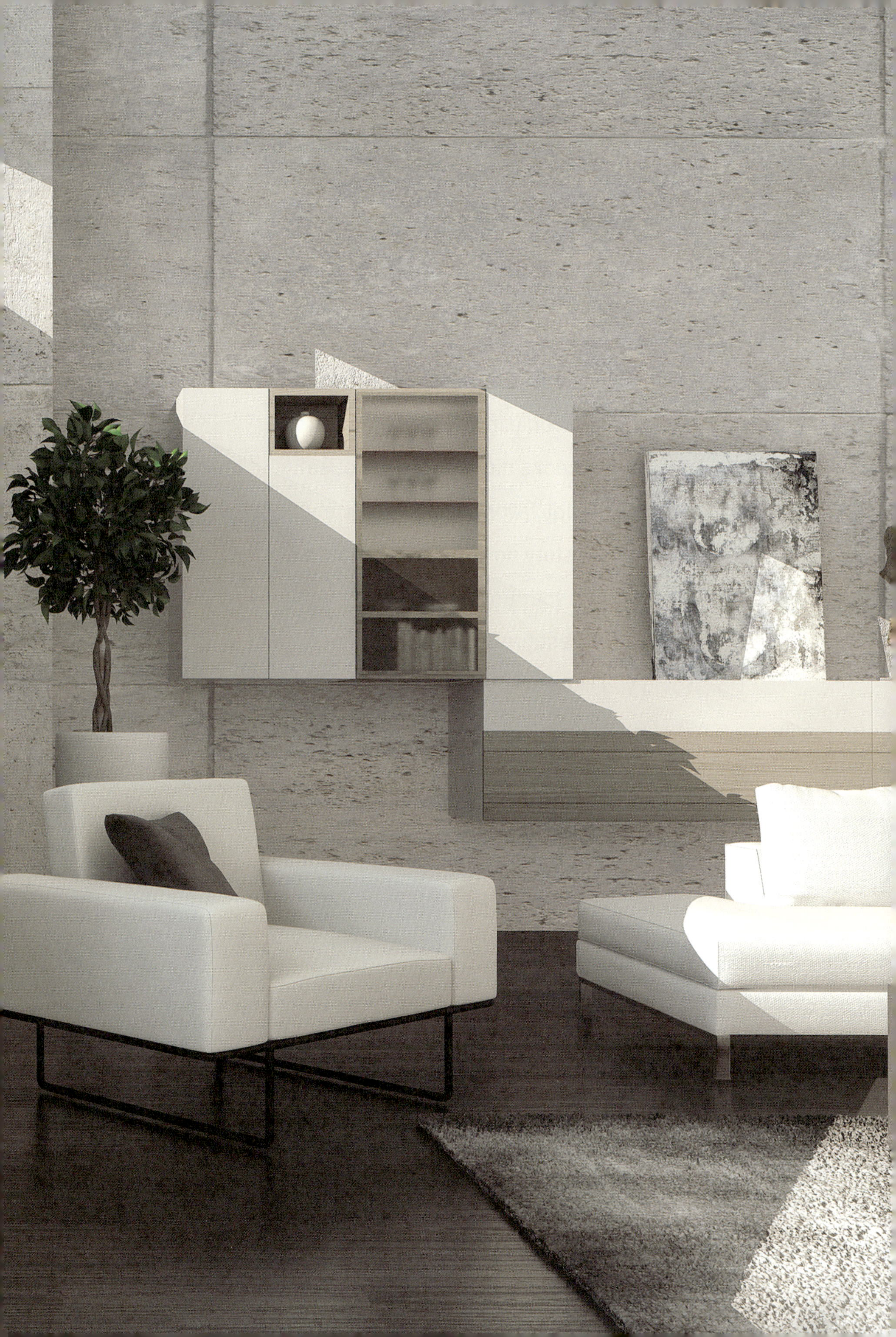

Unit 3

Who / Wearing / Personality
誰/穿著/形容個性、習性、天分

請至 MOSME 觀看教學影片

Core questions :

Q1. How many people are there in your family? Who are they?

Who are the people in your family?

Q2. Who usually cooks dinner at your house?

Q3. Who is your idol/favorite singer/movie star? Why?

Q4. Who in the history do you admire most? Why?

Q5. Tell me about your English teacher.

Who is your best friend? Describe him or her.

Q6. Would you like to be a teacher? Why or why not?

What do you want to be in the future? Why?

Q7. What do you wear?

What do you like to wear?

Q8. Do you have any bad habits? What are they?

Q9. Do you have any special skills or talents?

Unit 3 Who / Wearing / Personality | 23

Ms.Tips & Ponyo's daily conversation

How many people are there in your family?

Who are they?

There are three people in my family

Father

Sister

including my father, my little sister and I.

My father is a laborer.

He is kind, honest and hard-working.

My little sister is adorable and has rosy plump cheeks.

Words to use

1 Appearance 外貌

| tall 高 | short 矮 | fat 胖 | thin 瘦 |

| slender 苗條的 | slim 纖細的 | plump 豐滿的 | charming 有魅力 | attractive 吸引力的 |

|  handsome 帥氣的 | beautiful 美麗的 | graceful/elegant 優雅的 | strong 強壯的 |

| muscular 肌肉的 | overweight 過重的 | chubby 圓嘟嘟的 | rosy plump cheeks 紅潤豐滿的臉頰 |

| gorgeous 燦爛豔麗的 | cheerful 開心的 |  cute/adorable 可愛的 |

2 Personality 個性

| kind 善良的 | nice 好的 | friendly 友善的 | excellent 優秀的 | brilliant 傑出的 |

| smart/clever/wise/intelligent 聰明的 | diligent/ hard-working 勤奮的 |

Unit 3 Who / Wearing / Personality   25

| out-going 外向的 | | humorous 幽默的 | shy 害羞的 | modest 謙虛的 |

| generous 慷慨的 | hospitable 好客的 | honest 誠實的 | loyal 忠誠的 |

| reliable 可信賴的 | responsible 負責的 | gentle 溫和的 | easy-going 隨和的 | |

| energetic 精力充沛的 | enthusiastic 熱忱的 | passionate 熱情的 | considerate/thoughtful 體貼的 |

認識完關於外貌與個性的單字後，請試著寫出關於介紹人的對話吧！

How to answer the question

Q1. How many people are there in your family? Who are they? Who are the people in your family?

> 註：前後人數要對應好。且回答時間有限，儘量不要把所有親朋好友都算進去。

Ans.1 There are five people in my family, including grandma, mother, two brothers and I. My grandma is a vegetable vendor in a market, and my mother is a nurse. My two brothers and I are students. Though arguing with each other occasionally, we lead a happy and content life.

Ans.2 My family is a small one. There are three people in my family, including my father, my little sister and I. My father is a laborer and my little sister is an elementary school student. My father is kind, honest and hard-working. My little sister is adorable and has rosy plump cheeks. Though not rich, we lead a peaceful and decent* life.

*decent 體面的

✏ It's your turn! Write your answer down below:

_____
_____
_____
_____
_____
_____
_____

Q2. Who usually cooks dinner at your house?

> 註：運用強調語氣句型：It is…that…

Ans.1 It is my grandma that/who cooks dinner at my house. My grandma was a good cook while she was young. She is good at cooking and always makes a lot of delicious and mouth-watering dishes. I am so grateful for her.

Ans.2 It is I that usually cook dinner at my house. Sometimes my father will cook dinner when I have to go to cram school. However, both my father and I are not so good at cooking. As a result, we may eat out at a near-by cafeteria or a noodle stand.

✎ **It's your turn! Write your answer down below:**

___
___
___
___
___
___
___

Q3. Who is your idol/favorite singer/movie star? Why?

Ans.1 My idol/movie star is Daniel Radcliffe, acting as Harry Potter in many movies. He is handsome, humorous and intelligent. He played the leading role in many popular movies, which hit the box office*.

*box office 票房
*hit the box office 叫座的、票房好的

Ans.2 My idol/favorite singer is A-mei. She is diligent, energetic and easy-going. She sang a lot of popular songs and published quite a few wonderful albums. In addition, she has held many concerts and enchanted all her fans not only with her beautiful voice but also with her warm and elegant personality.

✏️ It's your turn! Write your answer down below:

___
___
___
___
___
___
___

Q4. Who in the history do you admire most? Why?

Ans.1 <mark>In my opinion</mark>, I admire Kongming* most because he is a great commander in post-Han dynasty* and is also a master of military strategy and politics. He is so wise that he had thought up special strategies to deal with some attacks from enemies.

*Kongming 孔明
*post-Han dynasty 後漢時期

Ans.2 <mark>From my point of view</mark>, I admire Qin Shihuang* most. He is the founder of Qin dynasty and the first emperor to unite China. During his reign*, he greatly expanded the size of the Chinese territory, and united several state walls into a single Great Wall, which is one of the wonders in the world.

*Qin Shihuang 秦始皇
*reign 統治時期

✏️ **It's your turn! Write your answer down below:**

Q5. Tell me about your English teacher.
Who is your best friend? Describe him or her.

Ans.1 My English teacher is Judy. She is graceful, nightlight and easy-going. She is good at encouraging students to learn English well. ==In addition==, she is like a friend of mine, accompanying me when I am frustrated or in bad mood.

Ans.2 My best friend is Jimmy. He is muscular, tall and modest. Though he is not good at schoolwork, he is a great basketball player. I sometimes play basketball with him after school or on the weekend. He is also a good listener, so I usually have a nice chat with him when I am depressed.

✏️ **It's your turn! Write your answer down below:**

___
___
___
___
___
___
___

Q6. Would you like to be a teacher? Why or why not?

What do you want to be in the future? Why?

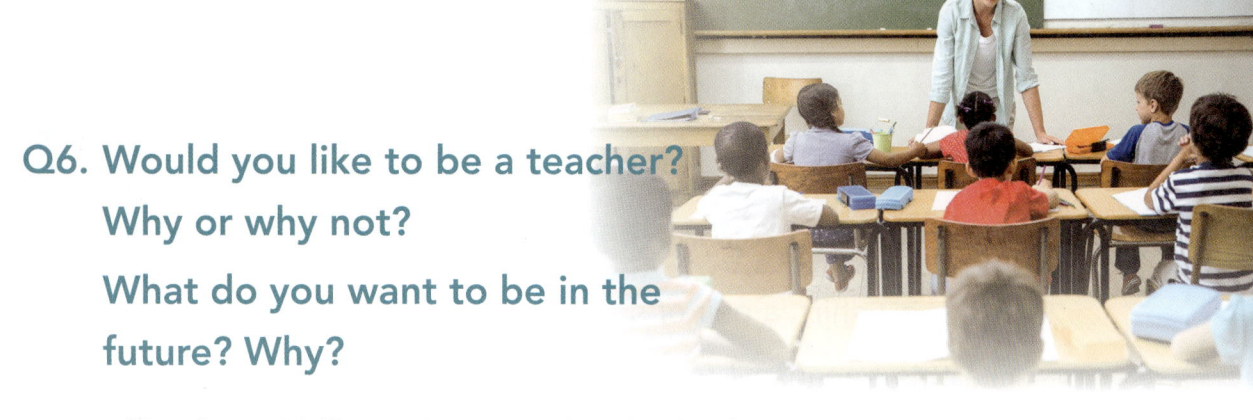

Ans.1 Yes, I would like to be a teacher in the future because my English teacher is my idol and I want to be like him one day. He is humorous, generous and energetic. English is my favorite subject. I enjoy his class very much and would like to be an English teacher like him.

Ans.2 No, I don't want to be a teacher because I want to be a policeman in the future. I am not so good at schoolwork and being a teacher will be a difficult task for me. A policeman can help people with a lot of difficulties, such as protecting good people from harm and putting bad guys into the prison. For me, being a policeman is the most wonderful life-long career. I hope I can make it one day.

✏ **It's your turn! Write your answer down below:**

Q7. What do you wear?
What do you like to wear?

Ans.1 I wear a T-shirt, a pair of shorts and sneakers. I usually like to wear like this because I feel most comfortable and relaxed. I can go biking or play sports by wearing like this.

Ans.2 I like to wear a dress or a suit with high-heels because I look most charming and slender when I am dressed like this. Looking beautiful makes me feel confident either in public places or in myself, which is very important to me.

✏ It's your turn! Write your answer down below:

Q8. Do you have any bad habits? What are they?

Ans.1 Yes, I have quite a few bad habits. First of all, I am usually late for school and make my teachers angry at me. In addition, I sometimes forget to do my homework and fail to pass the exam. The worst one is that I am a lazy student and don't focus on my studies. I hope I can get rid of them one day.

Ans.2 Yes, I have several bad habits. I spent too much money shopping online casually. What's worse, I spent too much time playing mobile games. I think I am an Internet addict. I know they are bad habits and I will try my best to quit them.

✏ It's your turn! Write your answer down below:

Q9. Do you have any special skills or talents?

> 註：Do you…? 簡答句：Yes, I do.(O) Yes, I have.(X)

Ans.1 Yes, I do. I can play badminton well and have won several medals. Badminton is my favorite sports. What's more, I can play the guitar well. I like to play the guitar with my friend singing songs around me. Playing badminton and the guitar are also my favorite recreation in my free time.

Ans.2 Yes, I do. I can swim very well. I can swim like a fish in the water and won't feel tired. In addition, I am good at drawing. I have learned drawing for more than ten years and now I can draw very well. In my leisure time, I usually go out drawing in a park or in the mountains. By the way, I can run fast. I am the fastest runner in my class.

✏ It's your turn! Write your answer down below:

_____
_____
_____
_____
_____
_____
_____

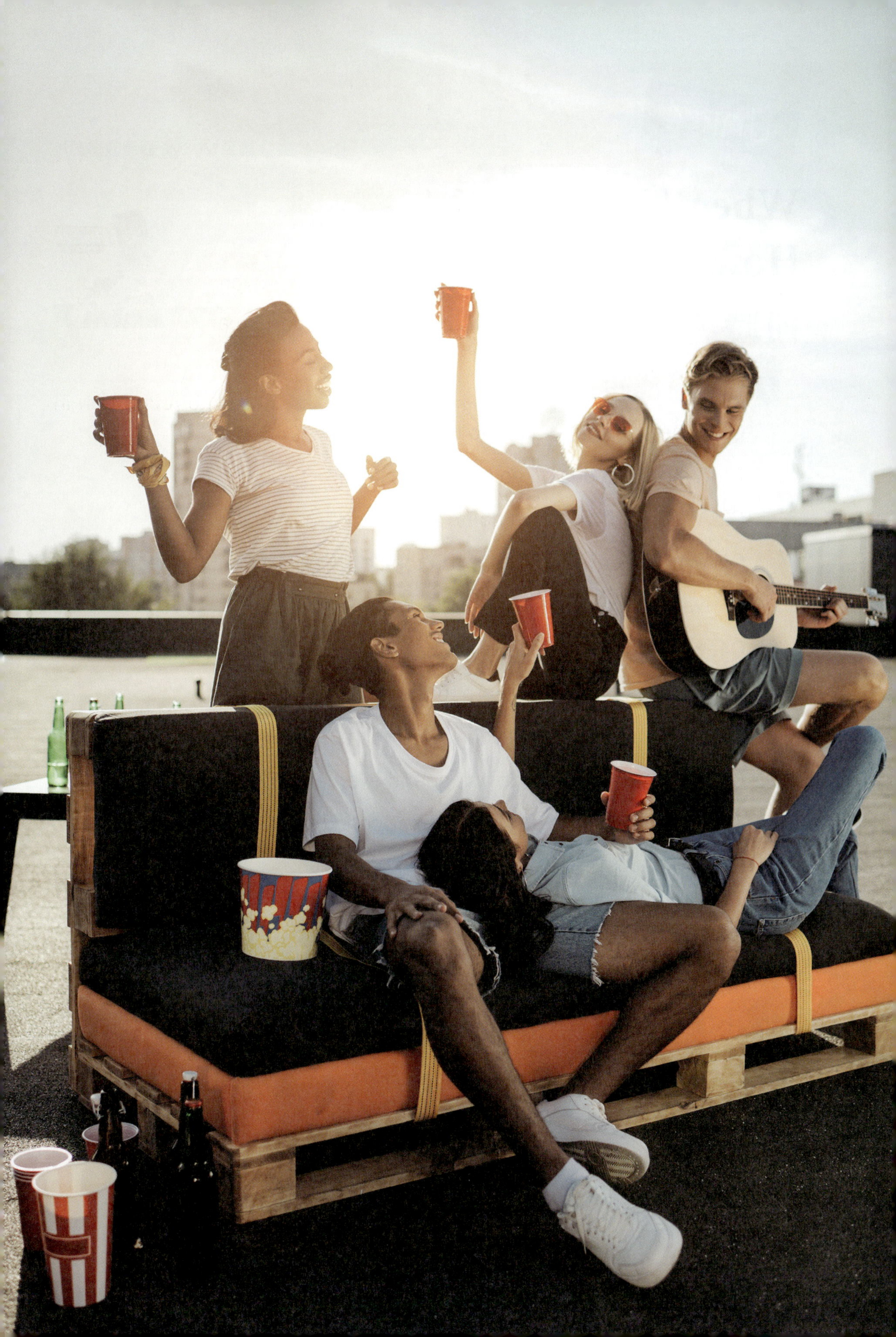

Unit 4

When / How long? / How much?

何時 / 多久？/ 多少？

Core questions:

Q1. When do you usually go to bed?

What time do you go to bed at night?

Q2. When did you leave home today?

Q3. When was the last time you took a vacation/went to the movies/went to see a doctor?

Q4. How long did it take to get here?

Q5. How long have you learned English?

Q6. How long have you lived where you are living now?

Q7. How much money do you spend every week?

Q8. How much time do you usually spend on your cell phone every day?

請至 MOSME 觀看教學影片

Unit 4 When / How long? / How much? | 37

Ms.Tips & Ponyo's daily conversation

When was the last time you took a vacation?

June
July

The last time I took a vacation was last month.

I went to Japan with my uncle.

Japan is my favorite country.

It is famous for the architecture of many old temples.

In addition, its people have the reputation of being very polite and honest.

What will be asked?

When
何時
（注意答句與問句的時態要一致）

How long
多久、多長

How much (money/time)
多少錢、多少時間

答句 tips：答句要針對題目來做選擇使用。

How to answer the question

Q1. When do you usually go to bed?

What time do you go to bed at night?

Ans.1 I usually go to bed at 11 o'clock or at midnight. I am a senior of high school* and have to go to cram school on every typical school day. When I am back home, it is almost ten o'clock. I spend more than one hour doing my homework and taking a shower, and then go to bed. Therefore, it is usually near twelve o'clock when I go to bed.

*senior of high school 高三生

Ans.2 I usually go to bed at 10 o'clock. I am a seventh grader and my parents don't put much emphasis on my schoolwork. However, they insist that I should go to bed at ten for the sake of my health. Otherwise, I will play online games with friends all night!

✏️ **It's your turn! Write your answer down below:**

_____
_____
_____
_____
_____
_____
_____

Q2. When did you leave home today?

> 註：注意答句的時態為「過去式」。

Ans.1 I left home at six o'clock. I had to ride my bike to the bus stop and to take a bus here. I arrived here at seven and then I went to a nearby café to grab a bite. Before taking this exam, I tried to keep calm in order to pass it and get the certificate.

Ans.2 I left home at one o'clock after finishing my lunch at home. My elder sister can ride a motorcycle and she kindly offered me a ride here. She waited for me outside the building when I took this oral exam. After the test, we will go shopping in the department store together.

✎ It's your turn! Write your answer down below:

___
___
___
___
___
___
___

Q3. When **was** the last time you took a vacation/went to the movies/went to see a doctor?

> 註：可以將 U2-Q4 的 Ans. 1 應用在此處。

Ans.1 The last time I took a vacation was last month. I went to Japan with my uncle. Japan is my favorite country. It is famous for the architecture of many old temples. In addition, its people have the reputation* of being very polite and honest. By the way, I like traditional Japanese clothes because they are graceful and elegant.

*reputation 聲譽

Ans.2 The last time I went to the movies was last Monday. I like to see sci-fi movie, and there was a popular one hitting the box office. I went to see that movie with my classmate after school last Monday. It was exciting, interesting and wonderful. I think I would like to see it again.

Ans.3 The last time I **went** to see a doctor **was** last Christmas. It **was** originally a merry time for family members. We **had** a feast, but I **ate** too much and **had** a stomachache. I **ended** up staying overnight in the hospital.

✏️ **It's your turn! Write your answer down below:**

Q4. How long did it take to get here?

> 註：可以將 U4-Q2 的 Ans.1 應用在此處。

Ans.1 It took about one hour to get here. This morning, I left home at six o'clock. I had to ride my bike to the bus stop and to take a bus here. I arrived here at seven and then I went to a nearby café to grab a bite. Before taking this exam, I tried to keep calm in order to pass it and get the certificate.

Ans.2 It took about 10 minutes to get here. My elder sister can ride a motorcycle and she kindly offered me a ride here. She waited for me outside the building when I took this oral exam. After the test, we will go shopping in the department store together.

✏️ **It's your turn! Write your answer down below:**

_____
_____
_____
_____
_____
_____
_____

Q5. How long **have you learned** English?

> 註：注意答句的時態為「現在完成式」。

Ans.1　I **have learned** English for three years. When I was a fourth grader, I started to go to a cram school for learning English. Three years past, and now I am a seventh grader. I have learned some basic English grammar and words. I hope I can pass this oral exam and get the certificate.

I have learned English for...

Ans.2　I **have learned** English for more than ten years since I was a child. My parents put a lot of emphasis on my English learning, so they employed a tutor to come to my house to teach me English. Now I have much interest and confidence in English. I hope I can pass this oral exam and get the certificate.

✎ It's your turn! Write your answer down below:

Q6. How long **have you lived** where you are living now?

> 註：可以將 U2-Q1 與 Q2 的 Ans.1 應用在此處。

Ans.1 I **have lived** in Tainan for more than seven years. My family moved here when I went to elementary school. Tainan is located in southern Taiwan and is famous for its traditional snacks. We especially like to eat stinky tofu, which is delicious and yummy.

Ans.2 I **have lived** in Taipei since I was born. Taipei is located in northern Taiwan and is the biggest city in Taiwan. It is famous for its convenient public transportation. People can take the MRT or buses to go to school or work.

✏ It's your turn! Write your answer down below:

Q7. How much money do you spend every week?

> 註：回答金額之後，可加入「買什麼」。

Ans.1 I spend about 200 NT dollars per week. I usually buy some bread and milk for my breakfast. If I don't spend all the money, I will save it as my pocket money.

Ans.2 I spend more than 500 NT dollars every week. I have to take a bus to school and back home. After school, I often eat out at a nearby stand for dinner and then I go to a cram school. On the weekend, I usually go shopping with my sister or go to the movies with my friends.

✎ It's your turn! Write your answer down below:

Q8. How much time do you usually spend on your cell phone every day?

> 註：回答「時間」之後，可加入「做什麼」。

Ans.1 I spend less than one hour on my cell phone. Now I am a senior of high school and have to concentrate on my studies in order to pass the Entrance Exam to go to a national university. Unless I need it to answer my mom's phone call or use it for looking for useful information for schoolwork, I don't want to waste time on it.

Ans.2 I spend more than 3 hours on my cell phone every day. In addition to checking my e-mails, I like to chat with friends online and play mobile games. It is interesting and offers me a lot of fun every day. Besides, using cell phones to surf on the Internet is more convenient than using computers. Cell phone is definitely the most wonderful invention in the world.

✏ It's your turn! Write your answer down below:

Unit 5

請至 MOSME 觀看教學影片

Frequency
頻率

❓ Core questions :

Q1. How often do you go shopping?

Q2. How often do you talk to your friends on the phone?

Q3. How often do you go to the zoo?

How often do you go to the movies?

Q4. How often do you eat at McDonald's?

你常去購物嗎?跟朋友都講多久電話呢?多久去一次動物園或是多久吃一次速食呢?想學會詢問各種事情的頻率就一起來看看吧!

Let's get started!

Unit 5 Frequency | 49

Ms.Tips & Ponyo's daily conversation

How often do you go shopping?

I go shopping once a week.

Sometimes I go to a nearby market with my mother,

and sometimes I go to a supermarket with friends.

I usually buy some snacks, chips, and chocolate.

They are delicious, wonderful and yummy.

Words to use

1 Frequency 頻率

| always 總是 | usually 通常 | often 常常 | seldom 很少 | never 從不 |

| one time/once 一次 | two times/twice 兩次 |  three times 三次 |

| four times 四次 | once in a while/occasionally 偶而 |

> 答句tips：回答頻率之後，可加入「跟誰、去哪裡、買什麼、做什麼、吃什麼」＋感受。

2 Feelings 感受

| interesting 有趣的 | exciting 振奮的 |  wonderful 很棒的 | marvelous 妙極了 |

|  a lot of fun 好玩 | pleasant 宜人的 | enjoyable 愉快的 |

| make me happy / relaxed 使我開心 / 放鬆 |  get rid of daily trifles 忘卻日常瑣事 |

Unit 5 Frequency   51

3 Taste 味道

delicious 可口的	yummy 好吃的	tasty 美味的	sour 酸的

sweet 甜的	bitter 苦的	spicy 辣的	mouth-watering 垂涎的

試著寫出一小段對話，來詢問對方多久去一次哪裡，或是多久吃一次某家餐廳吧！

How to answer the question

Q1. How often do you go shopping?

Ans.1 I go shopping once a week. Sometimes I go to a nearby market with my mother, and sometimes I go to a supermarket with friends. I usually buy some snacks, chips, and chocolate. They are delicious, wonderful and yummy.

Ans.2 I go shopping three times a week. I usually go to a traditional market to buy some vegetables, fruit, meat and bread. I buy them to prepare for dinner for my family. I can buy a variety of food and groceries in that traditional market. It is really a wonderful place for people to buy daily necessities.

✏️ **It's your turn! Write your answer down below:**

_____
_____
_____
_____
_____
_____
_____

Q2. How often do you talk to your friends on the phone?

Ans.1 I talk to my friends on the phone every day. We usually talk a lot about our daily life, including school teachers, classmates, homework, and even daily trifles. Having a nice chat with friends on the phone is pleasant and makes me relaxed.

Ans.2 I seldom talk to my friends on the phone now. I am a senior of high school and have a lot of homework to do. Now, I have to concentrate on my studies and cannot afford the time to chat with friends over the phone.

✏️ **It's your turn! Write your answer down below:**

_____
_____
_____
_____
_____
_____
_____
_____

Q3. How often do you go to the zoo?
How often do you go to the movies?

Ans.1 I go to the zoo two times a year. The zoo is not far from my house, and I can take the MRT there. I usually go there with my neighbors. We are animal-lovers. It is interesting, exciting and wonderful for us to watch animals in the zoo.

Ans.2 I go to the movies every week. I usually go to the movie theater in the department store near my house. I go there by bike with my elder sister. Both of us are movie-goers. We enjoy watching horror movies and sci-fi movies. They are interesting, exciting and wonderful. Watching movies is a good way for us to get rid of the pressure from schoolwork.

It's your turn! Write your answer down below:

Q4. How often do you eat at McDonald's?

> 註：將 U2-Q3 的 Ans.1、Ans.2 應用在此處。

Ans.1 I go to McDonald's with my friends several times a week. We like fast food, such as friend chicken, French fries, and Cola. Eating too much of them is not good for our health. However, they are so yummy and tasty that we love them very much.

Ans.2 I seldom eat at McDonald's. Though fast food may be delicious and yummy, it is not good for our health. Instead, I prefer to go to a seafood restaurant. There are several seafood restaurants near my house because I live in a fish village near the ocean. While my parents are busy with work, they usually take me to one of the seafood restaurants to enjoy our dinner. Seafood, such as crabs, oyster omelet*, fish, shrimps, etc, is delicious but not very expensive. We often have a good time enjoying our dinner there.

*oyster omelet 蚵仔煎

✏ It's your turn! Write your answer down below:

_____
_____
_____
_____
_____

Unit 6

請至 MOSME 觀看教學影片

What to eat?
吃什麼？

? Core questions:

Q1. What did you have for breakfast this morning?

Q2. What is your favorite snack?

Q3. Do you like Japanese food? Why or why not?

想跟朋友聊聊今天早餐吃什麼，或是自己最喜歡吃的零食、喜不喜歡吃日式料理嗎？那就一起來學習相關的單字和回答吧！

GO! GO! GO!

Ms.Tips & Ponyo's daily conversation

What did you have for breakfast this morning?

I had a hamburger, French fries and a glass of milk.

I had my breakfast at a fast-food restaurant.

I prefer Western-style food.

They are tasty and yummy.

I feel great after having them for my breakfast.

Words to use

1 Food 食物

| steak 牛排 | pork chop 豬排 | lamb cutlet 小羊排 |  chicken cutlet 雞排 |

| fried chicken fillet 炸雞排 |  fried chicken 炸雞 | French fries 薯條 |

| hot dog 熱狗 | stinky tofu 臭豆腐 | meat ball soup 貢丸湯  |

| clam soup 蛤蜊湯 | coffin bread 棺材板 |  omelet 蛋餅 |

| oyster omelet 蚵仔煎 | beef noodles 牛肉麵 | fried rice noodles 炒米粉 |

| spaghetti 義大利麵 | fried rice/noodles 炒飯/麵 |  pickles 泡菜 |

| picked vegetables 醃製蔬菜 | hot pot 火鍋 | dumpling 水餃 |

Unit 6　What to eat?　59

| rice dumpling 粽子 |  | porridge 麥片粥 | congee 稀飯 | sushi 壽司 |

| sweet potato congee 地瓜粥 | wasabi 山葵 / 哇沙米 | mustard 芥末醬 |  |

| ramen 拉麵 | toast with peanut butter 花生土司 | steamed bun 饅頭 |

| soy-bean milk 豆漿 | pudding 布丁 | tofu pudding 豆花 |

2 Related words 相關字

| foodie 美食家 / 饕客 | delicacies 佳餚 | cuisine 菜餚 / 烹飪法 |  |

> 答句tips：回答吃什麼之後，可加入「何時、跟誰、在哪裡吃」＋ delicious/yummy/ tasty ＋ 感受。

How to answer the question

Q1. What did you have for breakfast this morning?

> 註：注意答句的時態為過去式

Ans.1 I had two bowls of sweet potato congee with several pickled vegetable and a glass of soy-bean milk. They are traditional Chinese food for breakfast. They are delicious and yummy. I am always energetic after eating such a wonderful breakfast.

Ans.2 I had a hamburger, French fries and a glass of milk. I had my breakfast at a fast-food restaurant. I prefer Western-style food. They are tasty and yummy. I feel great after having them for my breakfast.

✏️ **It's your turn! Write your answer down below:**

_____
_____
_____
_____
_____
_____

Q2. What is your favorite snack?

Ans.1 My favorite snack is tofu pudding. I usually have it at a food stand with my classmate after school on my way home. It is so sweet and yummy that I sometimes buy some home for my family.

Ans.2 My favorite snack is cheese cake. I usually eat it in a café near my school. It is so yummy and is popular with many customers. I prefer having it with a cup of black coffee and enjoy a wonderful afternoon tea time.

✏️ It's your turn! Write your answer down below:

_____
_____
_____
_____
_____
_____
_____

Q3. Do you like Japanese food? Why or why not?

> 註：Do you…?
> 簡答句：Yes, I do.(O)
> 　　　　Yes, I like.(X)

Ans.1 Yes, I do. I like Japanese food, especially sushi with wasabi. They are spicy and yummy. I go to a Japanese restaurant with my grandfather for dinner once in a while. We are foodies and like to try many foreign delicacies, and Japanese food is our favorite one.

Ans.2 No, I don't. I don't like Japanese food, because many Japanese food goes with wasabi, which is too spicy. I prefer our traditional Chinese food, such as oyster omelet and coffin bread. They are delicious and yummy. I usually eat them in a food stand near my house and enjoy a wonderful dinner time with my family.

✏️ **It's your turn! Write your answer down below:**

_____
_____
_____
_____
_____
_____
_____

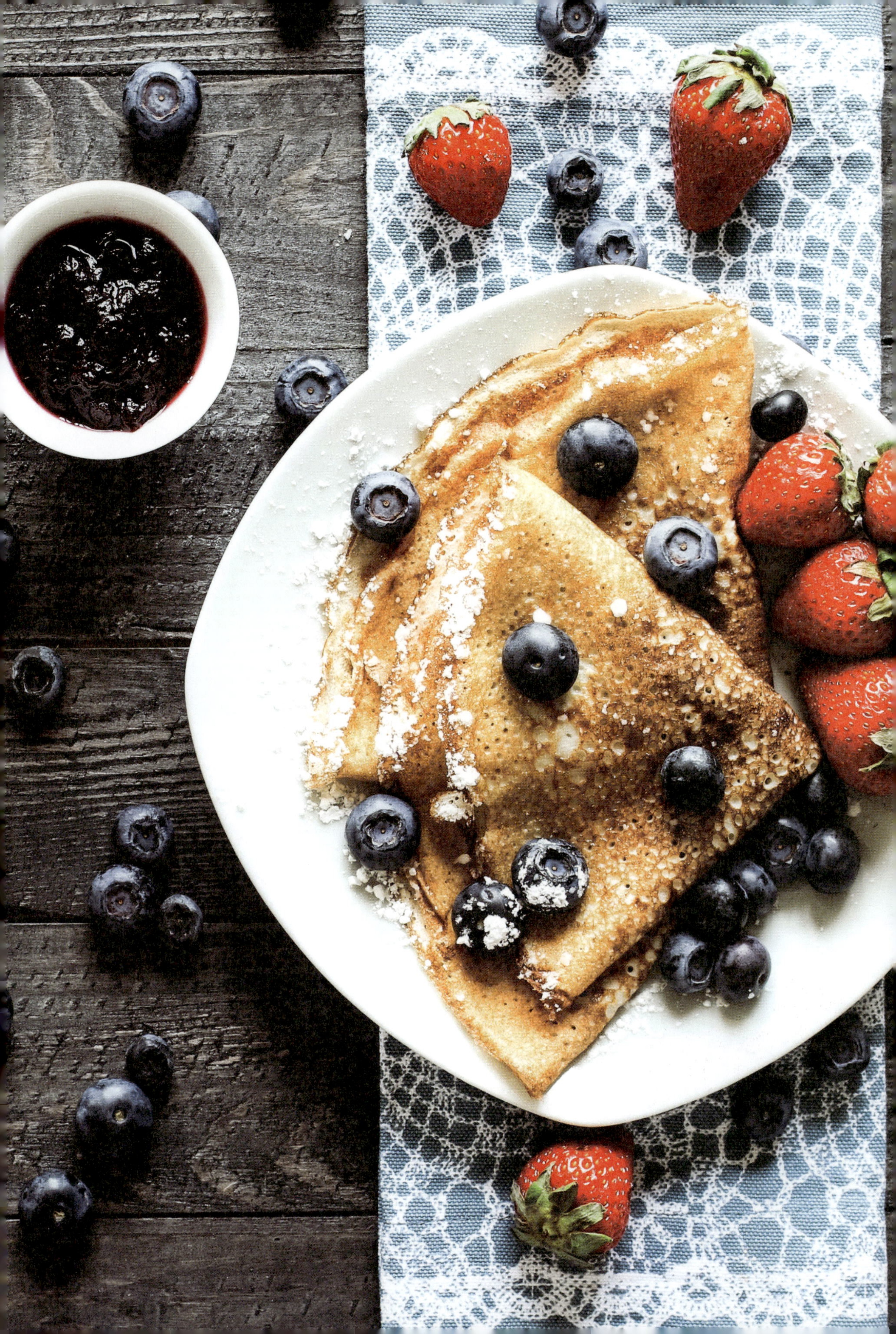

Unit 7

請至 MOSME 觀看教學影片

How to do it? / Methods
如何做？/ 問方法

? Core questions:

Q1. How do you go to school every day?

Q2. What are some good ways to learn English?

Q3. What can we do to save our earth?

Q4. What do you use a computer for?

你平常都如何上學呢？有什麼學英文的好方法嗎？要怎麼拯救我們的地球呢？你都用電腦來做什麼呢？熟悉了基本會話後就來學學其他話題，讓會話能力更近一步吧！

Ms. Tips & Ponyo's daily conversation

What can we do to save our earth?

In my opinion, we can reduce our garbage,

reuse the bags and …

recycle paper and bottles.

PAPER   BOTTLES

They are so-called 3R principles,

and are also useful ways to protect our environment and save our earth.

Words to use

1 Transportation 交通工具

walk/on foot	ride a bike/by bike
走路	騎腳踏車

ride a motorcycle/by motorcycle	take a train/by train
騎摩托車	搭火車

take a (school)bus/by (school) bus	take the MRT/by MRT
搭校車 / 公車	搭捷運

take a taxi/by taxi
搭計程車

drive a car/by car
開車

2 Related words 相關字

public transportation
公共運輸

3 Ways to learn English 學習英文的方法

| memorize English new words
記憶新的英文單字 | talk to foreigners
跟外國人說話 |

| listen to English songs
聽英文歌曲 | watch English movies
看英文電影 |

| look up English new words
查新的英文單字 | study abroad
去國外唸書 |

| read English novels
讀英文小說 | travel around the world
環遊全世界 |

4 Ways to protect the environment 保護環境的方法

| reduce the garbage
降低垃圾 | reuse shopping bags
再使用購物袋 |

| recycle paper and bottles
回收紙類和瓶子 | ride bikes
騎腳踏車 |

| turn off the lights and faucets
關燈和水龍頭 | take the public transportation
搭乘公共運輸 |

How to answer the question

Q1. How do you go to school every day?

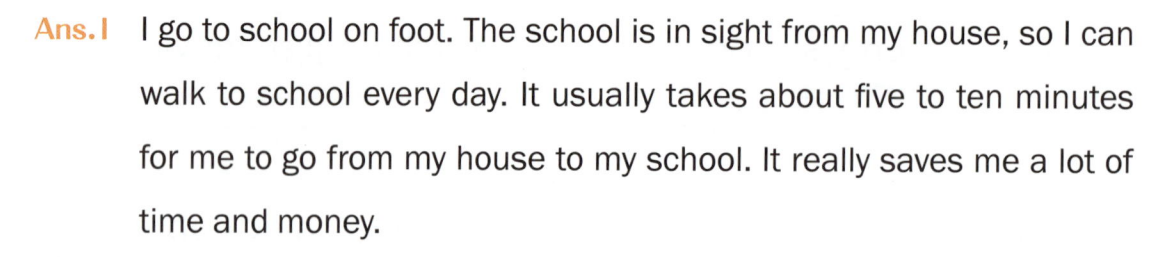

Ans.1 I go to school on foot. The school is in sight from my house, so I can walk to school every day. It usually takes about five to ten minutes for me to go from my house to my school. It really saves me a lot of time and money.

Ans.2 I go to school by school bus. The school is a little distant from my house, and I have to get up early to take the school bus to school. It usually takes me about one hour to go to school. When I get to school, it is 7 o'clock. I have another one hour to preview my lessons before the class begins at 8 o'clock.

✏️ **It's your turn! Write your answer down below:**

_____
_____
_____
_____
_____
_____
_____

Q2. What are some good ways to learn English?

> 註：重複題目的問句，可以為自己爭取幾秒思考的時間，盡量不要完全沒應答。

Ans.1 There are several good ways to learn English. First of all, we can memorize English new words as many as possible. Secondly, we can try to talk to foreigners. At last, we can listen to English songs or read English novels. They are useful ways to improve our English abilities.

Ans.2 There are several good ways to learn English. First of all, we can look up English new words in the dictionary as many as possible. In addition, going abroad for further study or traveling around the world is a useful way to learn English. At last, watching English movies is also helpful especially for the movie-goers. They are helpful ways to make our English better.

✏️ **It's your turn! Write your answer down below:**

_____
_____
_____
_____
_____

Q3. What can we do to save our earth?

With the increase/explosion of global population... 隨著全球人口的增加 / 遽增…	With the advance of science and technology... 隨著科技發展…

Ans.1 **With the increase of global population,** how to save our earth has become an important issue. In my opinion, we can reduce our garbage, reuse shopping bags and recycle paper and bottles. They are so-called* 3R principles, and are also useful ways to protect our environment and save our earth.

*so-called 所謂的

Ans.2 **With the explosion of global population,** how to save our earth has become a public concern. From my point of view, we can ride bikes or take the public transportation instead of riding motorcycles or driving cars. In addition, we can turn off the lights when leaving the room and turn off the faucets if we are not using it. They are helpful ways to protect our environment and save our earth.

✎ It's your turn! Write your answer down below:

_____

_____

_____

_____

_____

_____

Q4. What do you use a computer for?

Ans.1 With the advance of science and technology, computer has become a necessity in every family. I usually use it for receiving and sending e-mails, for looking for information for my homework, and mostly for playing online games. It is a useful tool for me.

Ans.2 With the advance of science and technology, computer has become a necessity for everyone. I use it for doing my homework, chatting with my classmates and keeping in touch with my friends in foreign countries. It is a helpful tool for people to contact with each other and do things more efficiently.

✏️ **It's your turn! Write your answer down below:**

_____

_____

_____

_____

_____

_____

_____

Unit 8

請至 MOSME 觀看教學影片

What do you do in your leisure time?

你在閒暇時做些什麼

❓ Core questions:

Q1. What did you do last Sunday?

What did you do yesterday?

Q2. How did you spend your last holiday?

Q3. What do you usually do when you are alone?

Q4. What do you like to do in your free time?

What do you usually do after school?

Q5. What do you do every day?

Q6. What is your favorite hobby?

Which sports do you like?

Q7. How do you usually celebrate your birthday?

Q8. What do your family members like to do?

Q9. What do people usually do on Christmas/New Year's Eve?

Q10. What will you do after the test?

What are you going to do tomorrow?

How are you going to spend next summer vacation?

Q11. What do you do when taking a train or bus?

Q12. If you had only 24 hours to live, what would you do?

Unit 8 What do you do in your leisure time? | 73

Ms.Tips & Ponyo's daily conversation

What did you do last Sunday?

I played badminton in a gym with my teammates in the early morning.

In the afternoon, I went shopping in a department store with my sister.

Then, in the evening, I played the piano alone at home.

Words to use

1 Ball games/Ball sports 球類運動

| Play+ | basketball 籃球 | baseball 棒球 | tennis 網球 |

| volleyball 排球 | badminton 羽球 | golf 高爾夫球 | soccer/football 足球 / 橄欖球 |

| table-tennis/ping-pong 桌球 | (ice) hockey （冰上）曲棍球 |

2 Sports/Activities 運動 / 活動

| Go+ | swimming 游泳 | mountain climbing 爬山 | jogging 慢跑 | hiking 健行 |

| camping 露營 | sightseeing 觀光 | shopping 逛街 | cycling 騎腳踏車 | boxing 拳擊 |

| go to the movies/see a movie 看電影 | go on a picnic/go picnicking 去野餐 |

| go to an amusement park/a zoo 去遊樂園 / 動物園 |

| Play+ | online/mobile games 網路遊戲 / 手遊 | chess/Chinese chess/cards 圍棋 / 象棋 / 撲克牌 |

practice tae kwon do/Tai Chi 跆拳道 / 太極拳	practice/perform aerobics 做有氧運動
practice/do yoga 做瑜珈	do weight training 做重訓

3 Instruments 樂器

Play the +	musical instruments 樂器	guitar 吉他	piano 鋼琴	violin 小提琴

organ 風琴	flute 笛子	saxophone 薩克斯風	trumpet 小號 / 喇叭

4 Related words 相關字

do regular exercise 規律運動	work out/exercise 運動	warm up 暖身

on the playground/ in the field 在操場	in the stadium 在體育場；競技場	in a gym 在健身房

athlete/player 運動員 / 球員	sportsman 喜歡做運動的人	sports day （學校）運動會

good for our body/mind/health 對身體 / 心靈 / 健康有益	keep in shape 保持身材（健康）

promote our health 促進我們的健康	lose weight 減重

註：回答「做什麼」之後，可加入「跟誰、何時、在哪裡」＋ good for our body/mind/health/promote our health/keep in shape + 感受（感受請參考 U5）。

How to answer the question

Q1. What did you do last Sunday?
What did you do yesterday?

> 註：注意答句的時態為「過去式」。

Ans.1 I played badminton in a gym with my teammates in the early morning. It helped me to lose some weight. In the afternoon, I went shopping in a department store with my sister. We bought some beautiful clothes for ourselves there. Then, in the evening, I played the piano alone at home, which is good for my mind. I had a wonderful time last Sunday.

Ans.2 Yesterday, I went to visit my grandparents with my family. My grandparents live in Tainan, which is located in southern Taiwan. Tainan is famous for its traditional snacks. We especially like to eat stinky tofu, which is delicious and yummy.

> 註：將 U2-Q1 的 Ans.1 應用在此處。

✏️ **It's your turn! Write your answer down below:**

_____
_____
_____
_____
_____
_____
_____

Q2. How did you spend your last holiday?

Ans.1 I went on a picnic with my family in a beautiful national park in the morning. The scenery is beautiful and pleasing. Then, we went to an amusement park in the afternoon. At last, we went to a fancy restaurant for dinner. We had a good time last holiday.

Ans.2 I went cycling with my brothers in the early morning in the countryside. In the afternoon, I played mobile games with them at home. Then, I did yoga with my mother. It was a wonderful and pleasant holiday for me.

✏️ **It's your turn! Write your answer down below:**

_____
_____
_____
_____
_____

Q3. What do you usually do when you are alone?

Ans.1 When I am alone, I usually ==play computer games==, ==read English novels== and ==work out in a gym==. Playing computer games is interesting and exciting. Reading English novels can promote my English abilities. Working out in a gym helps me keep in shape.

> 註：一次講三件事情，答句的內容才能豐富些。

Ans.2 When I am alone, I usually ==watch TV at home==, ==read fashion magazines in the library== or ==listen to English songs==. When watching TV, soap opera is my favorite program. It is interesting and exciting. Reading fashion magazines can help me catch up with the modern trend* and fashion. Listening to English songs helps me get rid of the pressure from daily life.

*trend 趨勢

✏️ **It's your turn! Write your answer down below:**

Q4. What do you like to do in your free time?
What do you usually do after school?

Ans.1 ==There are a lot of things I do in my free time==. I like to play mobile games, play table tennis and go shopping. I play mobile games when the Internet is available. I play table tennis with my friends after school. Besides, I like to go shopping with my girlfriend on the weekend.

Ans.2 ==There are a lot of things I do after school==. Sometimes I play basketball with my classmates after school on the playground, sometimes I go to the movies with my boyfriend if a new romantic movie is on and sometimes I play cards with my grandma at home. They are wonderful, exciting and good for my body and mind.

✏️ It's your turn! Write your answer down below:

_____
_____
_____
_____
_____
_____

Q5. What do you do every day?

Ans.1 <mark>There are a lot of things I do every day</mark>. I am a student now. Therefore, I go to school in the day time. After school, I do my homework at home. After dinner, I go to a gym to do some weight training to promote my body and health.

Ans.2 <mark>There are a lot of things I do every day</mark>. I go jogging in the early morning, play mobile games after school and do my homework after dinner every day. Going jogging is good for my health. Playing mobile games makes me relaxed. Doing my homework is a duty of being a student. They are my daily routine.

✎ **It's your turn! Write your answer down below:**

_____
_____
_____
_____
_____
_____
_____

Q6. What is your favorite hobby?
Which sports do you like?

by the way	In addition 此外
順帶一提	此外。

Ans.1 My favorite hobby is playing mobile games. There are a lot of online games. They are interesting and exciting. When I am in a bad mood or feel frustrated by schoolwork, I can play mobile games to relax myself. By the way, playing mobile games can keep in touch with my classmates because many of my classmates share the same interest as me.

Ans.2 I like to play volleyball. In my free time, I usually play volleyball with my neighbors in the field. It is interesting , exciting and wonderful. It is also good for my body and mind. By the way, I can make friends with students from other schools when playing volleyball.

✏️ It's your turn! Write your answer down below:

Q7. How do you usually celebrate your birthday?

Ans.1 I usually go shopping with my family and then we will go to a fancy restaurant for dinner. We like to order steak, pork chop and chicken cutlet. When we return home, my family may sing a birthday song to me and send me some birthday gifts. At last, we share a birthday cake together and have a nice time on my birthday.

Ans.2 I usually go to the movies with my friends and then we will go to a seafood restaurant. I like seafood very much, such as crabs, oyster omelet, fish, shrimps, etc. They are delicious but not very expensive. At last, we often eat a birthday cake. After my friends sing a birthday song to me, I will make three wishes.

> 註：將 U2-Q3 的 Ans.2 應用在此處。

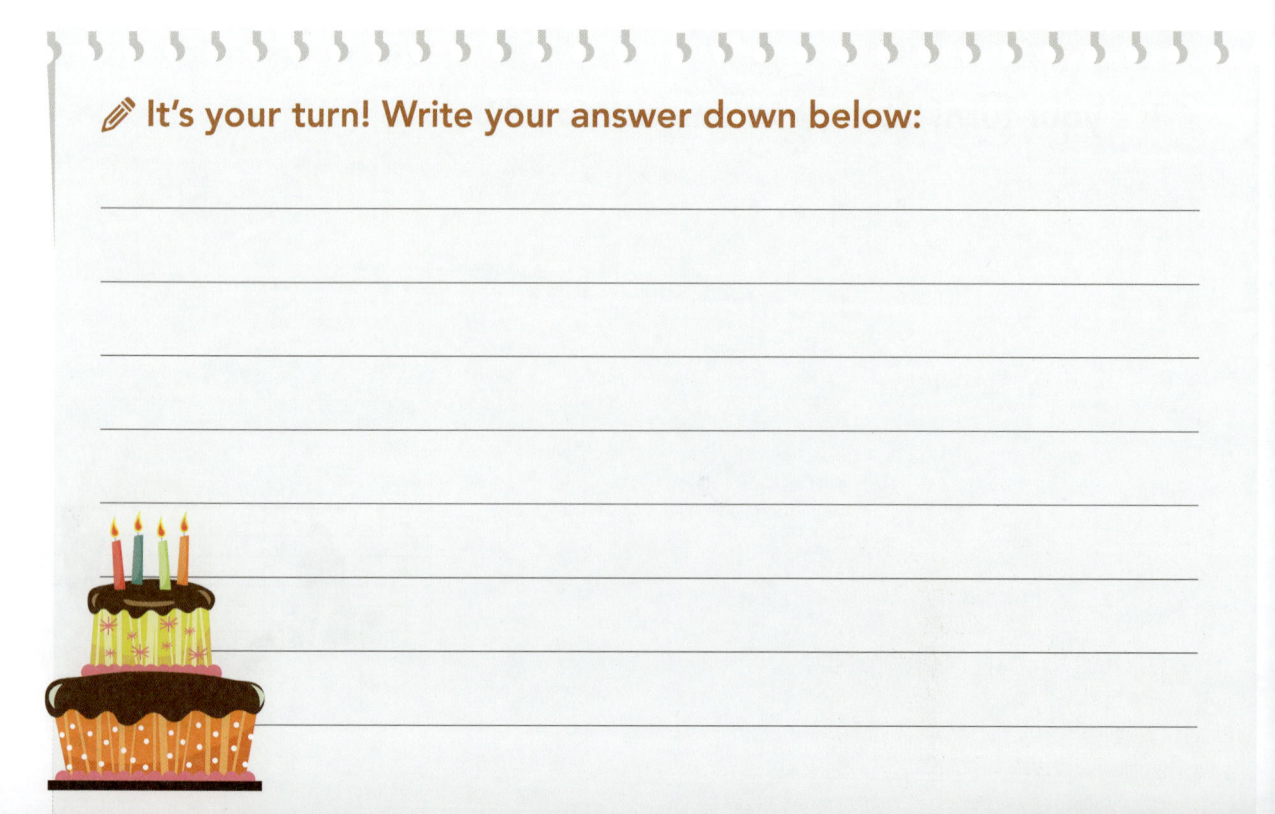

✏️ **It's your turn! Write your answer down below:**

Q8. What do your family members like to do?

Ans.1 There are four people in my family. My father is a worker and he likes to go jogging after work. My sister is a college student and she likes to play the violin on the weekend. My little brother is an elementary school student and he enjoys playing volleyball with his classmates after school.

Ans.2 There are three people in my family. My grandma likes to play online games at home and do yoga at a community activity center. My brother likes to go to the movies with his girlfriend and do some weight training. By the way, they both like to play Chinese chess with each other.

✏ It's your turn! Write your answer down below:

_____
_____
_____
_____
_____
_____
_____
_____
_____

Q9. What do people usually do on Christmas/Chinese New Year's Eve?

Ans.1 Christmas is on December twenty-fifth. People like to decorate their Christmas trees with some decorations, such as stars, bells, gifts and some little stuff. People usually exchange cards or gifts with each other. At night, people will sing Christmas songs to bless for themselves and others.

Ans.2 People usually have a feast and stay up all nights on Chinese New Year's Eve. They gather together on Chinese New Year's Eve and children often get red envelopes from the elder members of their family. They may stay up playing cards or playing mahjong*. What's important of all is to wish each other a good coming year.

*mahjong 麻將

✏ **It's your turn! Write your answer down below:**

Q10. What will you do after the test?
What are you going to do tomorrow?
How are you going to spend next summer vacation?

> 註：注意問答句的時態為「未來式」。
> 可將 U2-Q3、Q1 的 Ans.1 改成「未來式」，應用在此處。

Ans.1   I am going to go to McDonald's with my friends. We like fast food, such as fried chicken, French fries, and Cola. Eating too much of them is not good for our health. However, they are so yummy and tasty that we love them very much.

Ans.2   Tomorrow, I am going to Kenting, which is located in the southern part of Taiwan. Kenting is famous for its wonderful weather and natural beauty. I will also go hiking in Kenting National Park and go to the sea for snorkeling.

Ans.3 I am *going to* go to Australia next summer vacation. There are many famous animals in Australia, such as koalas and kangaroos. They are unique to Australia and can't be found anywhere else. ==By the way==, they are so cute and interesting. I cannot wait for a trip to this country.

> 註：將 U2-Q4 的 Ans.3 應用在此處。

✎ It's your turn! Write your answer down below:

_____
_____
_____
_____
_____
_____
_____
_____

Q11. What do you do when taking a train or bus?

Ans.1 I have to take a school bus every day. On the bus, I usually play mobile games, surf the Internet, or listen to music. They are interesting, exciting and a lot of fun. They can make me happy and relaxed, too.

Ans.2 Well…when taking a bus , I usually read books and listen to music at the same time. I read English novels or listen to English songs in order to improve my English reading and listening skills. English is my favorite subject. By the way, my English teacher is intelligent, enthusiastic and humorous. I enjoy a lot in his English classes and gain a lot of confidence and knowledge from him.

> 註：若提到「科目」，可參考 U9-Q1 的 Ans1。

✏️ **It's your turn! Write your answer down below:**

_____
_____
_____
_____
_____
_____
_____

Q12. If you had only 24 hours to live, what **would** you do?

Ans.1 I would play mobile games with my sister, play Chinese chess with my mother, and play some piano songs for my family. My family is a small one. There are three people in my family, including my mother, my sister and I. Although we are not rich, we lead a content and happy life. To live with them is a blessing for me.

Ans.2 I would go sightseeing around our hometown with my family. Taitung is my hometown. It is located in eastern Taiwan. Taitung is famous for its hot springs, especially Jhihben hot springs and picturesque landscape. I was born in a peaceful village, Chishang and its rice production, such as meal box, is popular all over the island. I would miss it if I had only 24 hours to live.

✏️ **It's your turn! Write your answer down below:**

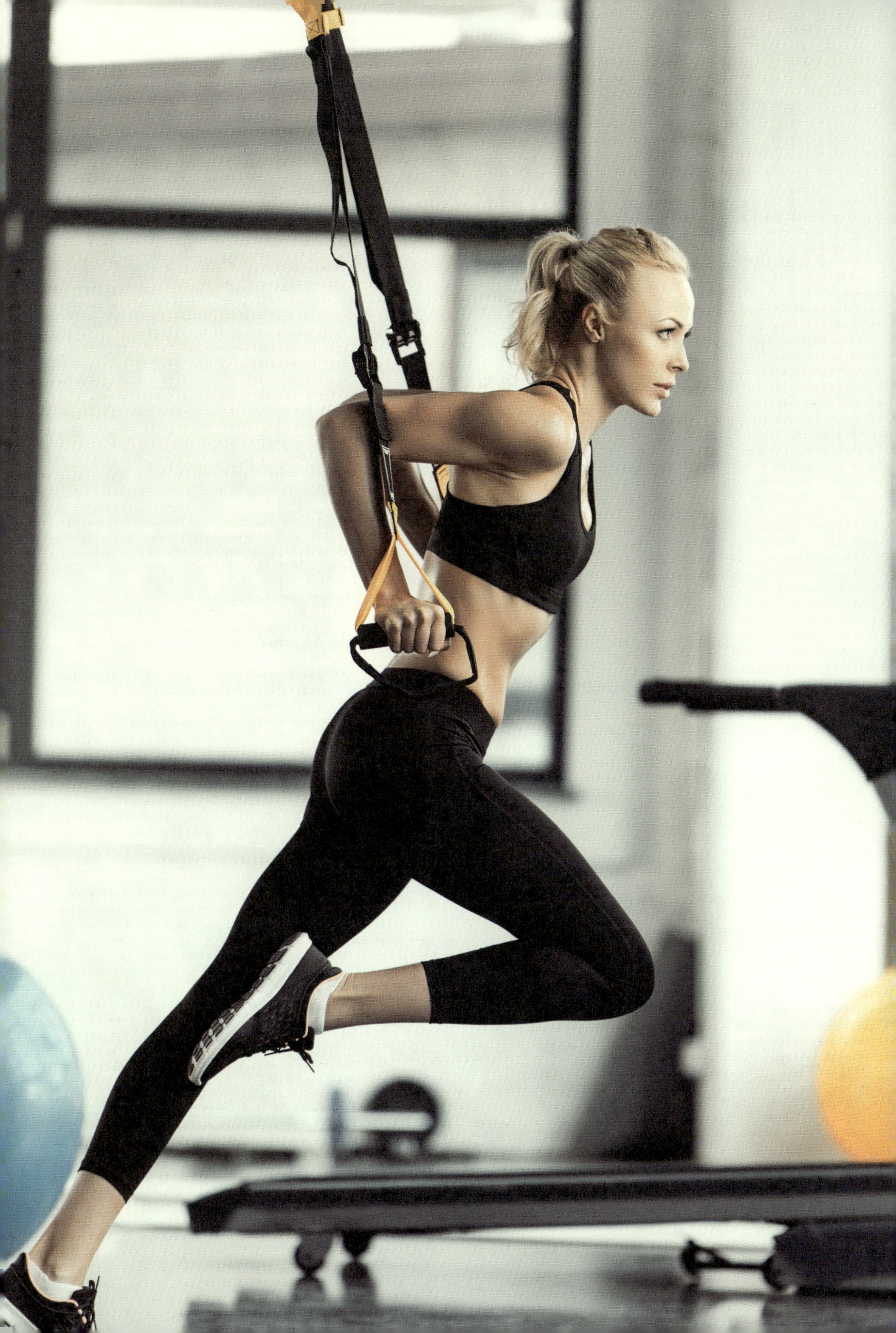

Unit 9

Likes and favorites
喜歡與最愛

請至 MOSME 觀看教學影片

❓ Core questions :

Q1. What is your favorite subject?

Q2. What is your favorite color? Why?

Q3. What kind of TV programs/movies do you like to watch?

　　Do you often go to the movies? Why?

Q4. Do you like to play computer games? Why or why not?

　　Do you play any video games when you are free?

Q5. Do you like swimming/riding a bicycle? Why?

Q6. Do you keep a pet? If not, what kind of animals do you prefer?

你喜歡什麼顏色？喜歡什麼科目呢？又或是你喜歡哪種電視節目、電影？喜歡寵物嗎？只要學完這單元就能輕鬆應答喔！快來一起看看吧！

Let's get started!

Ms.Tips & Ponyo's daily conversation

What is your favorite subject?

PE is my favorite subject.

I like to play badminton,

baseball, …

and to go swimming in the swimming pool.

Words to use

1 Subject 科目

| Chinese 國文 | English 英文 | mathematics (math) 數學 | arts 美術 |

| physical education (PE) 體育 | history 歷史  |

| science 自然 | social science 社會 | geography 地理 | biology 生物 |

2 Color 顏色

| red 紅 | orange 橙 | yellow 黃 | green 綠 | blue 藍 |

| indigo 靛 | purple 紫 | black 黑 | white 白 | gray/grey 灰 |

3 Program 電視節目

| cartoon 卡通 | news 新聞 |  soap operas 連續劇 | variety shows 綜藝節目 |

| reality shows 實境節目 | game shows 競賽節目 | talent shows 才藝節目 | talk shows 談話性節目 |

| TV series 電視影集 | ancient Chinese dramas/Mainland dramas 古裝劇 / 大陸劇 |

| opera 戲劇 |  Korean dramas 韓劇 |

| Discovery Channel 探索頻道 | sports / movie /shopping channels 運動 / 電影 / 購物頻道 |

4 Film Genre 電影類別

| romance/horror/suspense movie 愛情文藝 / 恐怖 / 懸疑片 |  thrillers 驚悚片 |

| action/fantasy movie 動作 / 奇幻片 | science-fiction movie (sci-fi movie) 科幻片 |

| animation/animated cartoon 動畫片 / 動畫卡通 | disaster movie 災難片 | war film 戰爭片 |

| drama 劇情片 | westerns 西部片 |  historical movie 歷史片 |

| martial arts 武俠片 | adventure movie 冒險片 |

5 Related words 相關字

| binge-watch(v.) 追劇 | comedy 喜劇 | tragedy 悲劇 | movie-goer 愛好電影的人 |

How to answer the question

Q1. What is your favorite subject?

> 註：喜歡這科目的原因如果是「老師／同學」，就可以用形容人「個性」的形容詞（請參考 U3）

Ans.1 English is my favorite subject. I like to read English books and watch English movies. *In addition*, my English teacher is intelligent, enthusiastic and humorous. He is always helpful whenever I meet some difficulties in English. I enjoy a lot in his English classes and gain a lot of confidence and knowledge from his teaching.

Ans.2 PE(Physical Education) is my favorite subject. I like to play badminton, baseball and to go swimming in the swimming pool. Doing exercise can help me keep in shape. *By the way*, my PE teacher is easy-going, generous and energetic. He teaches me how to play and swim well and helps me to develop good sportsmanship. I have a good time in PE classes.

✎ **It's your turn! Write your answer down below:**

Unit 9 Like and favorite | 95

Q2. What is your favorite color? Why?

Ans.1 I like green best because it is the color of grass. When it comes to green grass, I will think of my hometown, ==Taitung==. It is located in eastern Taiwan and is famous for its hot springs, especially Jhihben hot springs and picturesque landscape. I was born in a peaceful village, Chishang and its rice production, such as meal box, is popular all over the island.   註：將 U2-Q2 的 Ans.2 應用在此處。

Ans.2 I like the color, blue most. That's because it is the color of sky and the ocean. When it comes to the ocean, ==Kenting== National Park comes to my mind. Kenting National Park is located in the southern part of Taiwan and is famous for its wonderful weather and natural beauty. I can't help imagining going hiking there and going snorkeling in the ocean.

註：將 U2-Q1 的 Ans.1 應用在此處。

✏ It's your turn! Write your answer down below:

_____
_____
_____
_____
_____
_____

Q3. What kind of TV programs/movies do you like to watch? Do you often go to the movies? Why?

Ans.1 I like Discovery Channel. It introduces many kinds of animals and they are cute, unique, and interesting. It also informs people of some useful knowledge about our earth and other planets. As for me, I am curious about outer space because I want to be an astronaut in the future.

Ans.2 Yes, I do. I like to go to the movies. I enjoy watching action movies in particular. They are interesting, exciting and marvelous. They not only help me get rid of daily trifles but also offer me a lot of fun. By the way, my mom is a movie-goer and enjoy action movies, too. Our favorite action movie is Superman. We go to the movies once a week and have a lot of fun together.

✏ It's your turn! Write your answer down below:

_____
_____
_____
_____
_____
_____
_____
_____

Q4. Do you like to play computer games? Why or why not? Do you play any video games when you are free?

Ans.1 Yes, I do. I like to play computer games. There are a lot of games online. I can play it all day long and it won't bore me at all. I play computer games four times a week with my net friends and classmates. Computer games are interesting, exciting and wonderful. Playing computer games helps me get rid of the pressure from schoolwork and helps me relaxed.

Ans.2 No, I don't. I don't like to play computer games at all. It not only does harm to my eyes and health but also wastes time. Instead, I would rather read at home or play sports games outdoors. Reading offers me with a variety of knowledge to enrich my mind and playing sports strengthens my body.

> 註：提到「不喜歡玩」，除了提出原因之外，若還有時間，可以順便提出「喜歡什麼」。

Ans.3 Yes, I do. I like to play video games when I have free time. There are a lot of video games for me to choose from and I am good at playing them. I usually play them with my brother, who shares the same interest with me. Video games are exciting, interesting and great fun for both of us. What's important of all, they can help me get rid of daily trifles.

✏️ **It's your turn! Write your answer down below:**

_____
_____
_____
_____
_____
_____
_____
_____

Q5. Do you like swimming /riding a bicycle? Why?

> 註：答句可以應用「人、事、時、地、物」，例如跟誰、去哪裡、時間頻率、感受，若有時間，可以再加入「之後做什麼」。

Ans.1 Yes, I do. I like swimming. I am good at swimming and it is my favorite exercise. It is wonderful and good for my health. I usually go swimming in a swimming pool in a community activity center twice a week. Sometimes I go there with my mom, and sometimes I go with my neighbors. After swimming, we usually go to a nearby noodle stand to have a bowl of delicious beef noodles.

Ans.2 Yes, I do. Riding a bicycle is wonderful and good for our health, especially riding along the roads and the fields in the countryside. I live in Taipei, which is a big city with serious air and noise pollution. Once in a while, I will pay a visit to my grandparents, who live in Tainan County. When going bicycle riding, I can enjoy the natural beauty and picturesque landscape and have a lot of fun.

✏ It's your turn! Write your answer down below:

Q6. Do you keep a pet? If not, what kind of animals do you prefer?

Ans.1 Yes, I do. I keep a pet bird. Its name is Ponyo and it is cute, but noisy and naughty. Its feathers are green, with some yellow feathers around its neck and some red and blue feathers on its tail. In my free time, I like to ride a bicycle with it sitting on my shoulder. We both enjoy the natural beauty and picturesque landscape in the fields. I enjoy its company a lot and will take care of it for its lifetime.

Ans.2 No, I don't. My family don't allow me to keep any pet. However, if I could, I would like to keep a pet dog. Dogs are said to be loyal and be best friends to human beings. Some are little and cute, and some are big and can play tricks with their masters. One day, I hope to keep a big one, so I can go jogging with it every day.

✏️ **It's your turn! Write your answer down below:**

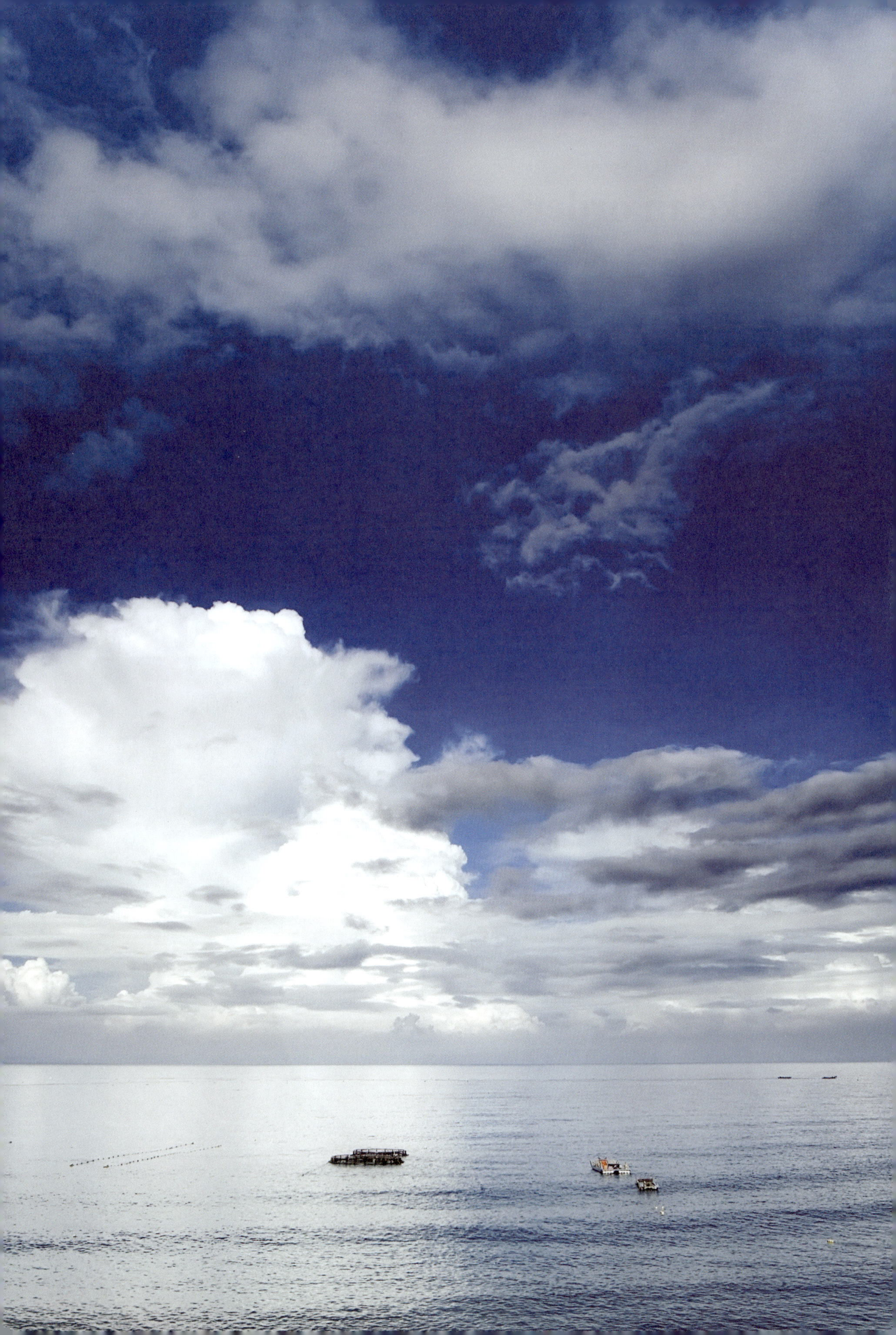

Unit 10

Make an order

點餐

請至 MOSME 觀看教學影片

❓ Core questions：

Q1. May I take/have your order?

How do you like your steak/eggs/drinks?

Q2. What do you usually have to go with the meat?

Q3. How sweet do you like?

How about the ice?

不論是出國玩或是招待外國朋友去餐廳用餐，都很可能會需要用英文點餐、翻譯，因此本章將介紹有關點餐的實用英文口說，從西式排餐、配料到飲料調整，實用又簡單，一起來看看吧！

Let's go!

Ms.Tips & Ponyo's daily conversation

May I take your order?

Yes, I'll have a T-bone steak.

How do you like it cooked?

I like it (cooked) medium-rare.

I'd like two cups of bubble milk tea.

How sweet do you like?

Regular.

How about the ice?

half.

And for here or to go?

To go, please.

Words to use

1 Main course/Main dish/ Entrée 主菜

| Ribeye 肋眼 | Filet 菲力 |  | short rib 牛小排 | blade 板腱 |

| New York 紐約客 | T-bone 丁骨 | Sirloin 沙朗 |

2 Degree of cooking 烹飪熟度

- well-done 全熟
- medium-well 七分熟 
- medium 五分熟 
- medium-rare 三分熟 
- rare 一分熟 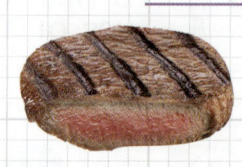

3 Sauce 醬汁

| wild mushroom sauce 蘑菇醬 | black pepper sauce 黑胡椒醬 | A1 steak sauce A1 牛排醬 |

| ketchup 蕃茄醬 | crispy garlic slice 香酥蒜片 | sea salt 海鹽 | pink salt 玫瑰鹽 |

4 Side dishes 配菜

mashed potato	baked potato	grilled tomato
馬鈴薯泥	烤馬鈴薯	焗烤蕃茄

corn	broccoli	onion
玉米	花椰菜	洋蔥

5 Dessert 甜點

brownie
布朗尼

sundae
聖代

cheese cake
起司蛋糕

fruit jelly
水果果凍

muffin
馬芬 / 小鬆餅

waffle/pancake
鬆餅 / 煎餅

scone
司康

milk shake
奶昔

cheese souffle
起司蛋奶酥

macaron
馬卡龍

brûlée
烤布蕾

marshmallow
棉花糖

Unit 10　Make an order　105

6 Egg 蛋

hard-boiled egg 全熟白煮蛋	poached egg 醣心蛋	scrambled egg 炒蛋

sunnyside-up egg 煎一邊的蛋	omelette 煎蛋捲	fried egg 煎蛋

over-easy egg 雙面煎得半生熟的荷包蛋	over-medium egg 雙面煎得五分熟	over-hard egg 雙面煎得全熟

with yolk hard/soft
蛋黃熟 / 半熟

7 Tea 茶

green tea 綠茶	black tea 紅茶	earl grey tea 伯爵紅茶	Assam black tea 阿薩姆紅茶

Ceylon black tea 錫蘭紅茶	jasmine tea 茉莉花茶	lemon tea 檸檬茶

pearl milk tea/bubble milk tea/tapioca milk tea 珍珠奶茶	milk tea 奶茶

peppermint tea 薄荷茶	oolong tea 烏龍茶	Pu-erh tea 普洱茶

light oolong tea 青茶	ginger tea 薑茶

Unit 10 Make an order   107

8 Amount of ice 冰塊

| With + | extra ice 加冰 | regular ice 正常冰 | easy/light ice 少冰 | ice free 去冰 |

9 Sweetness level 甜度

| With + | extra sugar 加糖 | regular sugar 正常甜 | less sugar 少糖 | half sugar 半糖 |

| quarter/light sugar 微糖 | sugar free 無糖 |

10 Ingredients 配料

| With + | boba 波霸 | tapioca peals/bubble 珍珠 | flan/pudding 焦糖布丁 / 布丁 |

| taro balls 芋圓 | grassy jelly 仙草 | coconut jelly 椰果 |

| thick rice noodles 米苔目 |

11 Alcohol 酒類

| wine 葡萄酒 | red wine 紅酒 | white wine 白酒 | beer 啤酒 | wheat beer 小麥啤酒 |

| rice wine 米酒 | plum wine 梅酒 | sparkling wine 氣泡酒 | Champaign 香檳 |

12 Liquor 烈酒

| tequila 龍舌蘭 | whisky 威士忌 | vodka 伏特加 | rum 萊姆 |

| gin 琴酒 | brandy 白蘭地 | sake 日本清酒 |

13 Cocktail 雞尾酒

| martini 馬丁尼 | bloody mary 血腥瑪麗 | long island ice tea 長島冰茶 | margarita 瑪格麗特 |

14 Amout of ice 冰塊量

| neat 不加冰塊 | on the rocks 加冰塊 |

15 Related words/terms 相關用字 / 用語

| for here 內用 | to go 外帶 | It is my treat. 我請客 | Check, please. 埋單 | Go Dutch. 各付各的 |

1. How sweet do you like? How about the sugar?（問甜度）
2. How do you like to do for the ice? How about the ice?（問冰塊）
3. I want to place a delivery order. 我想訂外送。
4. Can you give me a doggy bag? 我可以給我打包的袋子嗎？
5. Can you help me wrap this leftover up?
   可以幫我把剩餘的食物打包嗎？

How to answer the question

**Q1. May I take/have your oder?
How do you like your steak/
eggs/drinks?**

Dialogue 1:

Waiter: Hello, I am Jay. I'll be your waiter today. Can I get you something to drink?

Ponyo: I'll have a diet Coke.

Waiter: Good. I'll be right back.

(Five minutes later)

Waiter: Are you ready to order?

Ponyo: Well...I don't know. Do you have any recommendation?

Waiter: The peppered chicken and the New York steak are popular here.

Ponyo: Thank you. I will think about it. Just a moment.

Waiter: No problem. Take your time. I'll be back soon.

Dialogue 2:

Waitress: Hi, I am Lily. I'll be your waitress today. Can I get you anything to drink?

Ms. Tips: Water, please.

Waitress: Would you like sparkling water or regular?

Ms. Tips: Regular, Please

Waitress: Great. I'll be back soon.

(Three minutes later)

Waitress: May I take your order?

Ms. Tips: Yes, I'll have a T-bone steak.
Waitress: How do you like it cooked?
Ms. Tips: I like it (cooked) medium-rare.
Waitress: And what kind of dressing would you like?
Ms. Tips: What kind do you have?
Waitress: We have wild mushroom sauce and black pepper sauce.
Ms. Tips: Black pepper sauce.
Waitress: And what do you like to go with your steak? We have grilled tomatoes, a baked potato and mashed potato.
Ms. Tips: I would like grilled tomatoes.
Waitress: All right. That's a T-bone steak, medium-rare cooked, with black pepper sauce. Grilled tomatoes as side dishes to go with the meat.

✎ It's your turn! Write your answer down below:

Q2. What do you usually have to go with the meat?

Ans.1 I like potatoes. Therefore, I usually have potato chips, mashed potato or baked potato to go with my T-bone steak. For me, any kind of potatoes is delicious, tasty and makes my mouth water. I can't resist it.

Ans.2 I usually order some corns and broccoli to go with the meat. Vegetables are good for health. In addition, the fresh color of the vegetables will increase my appetite.

✏️ It's your turn! Write your answer down below:

___
___
___
___
___
___
___

Q3. How sweet do you like?
How about the ice?

Dialogue 1

Waiter/Waitress: May I take your order?

Ponyo: Yes. I'd like two cups of pearl milk tea.

Waiter/Waitress: How sweet do you like?

Ponyo: Regular.

Waiter/Waitress: How about the ice?

Ponyo: Half.

Waiter/Waitress: And for here or to go?

Ponyo: For here, please.

✏️ **It's your turn! Write your answer down below:**

_____
_____
_____
_____
_____
_____

Dialogue 2

Waiter/Waitress: Next, please. What would you like to have, ma'am?

Ms. Tips: Two cups of Assam black tea to go.

Waiter/Waitress: How about the sugar?

Ms. Tips: One is half sugar, and the other is sugar free.

Waiter/Waitress: And how do you like to do for the ice?

Ms. Tips: Light ice, please.

Waiter/Waitress: No problem. Please wait a moment and your drinks will be ready soon.

✏️ **It's your turn! Write your answer down below:**

Unit 11

Make a phone call
電話用語

Core conversation:

Conversation 1 : This is Ms. Tips speaking.

Conversation 2 : I will put her on.

Conversation 3 : I'll transfer your call to Ms. Tips.

Conversation 4 : I can't get through to her. The line is busy.

Conversation 5 : Ms. Tips is out at the moment.

Conversation 6 : I'm afraid you have the wrong number.

請至 MOSME 觀看教學影片

在日常生活中，不論是在家或工作，常常會接到電話，當對方要找的人不在，或就是你本人時要怎麼回答呢？如果要找的人不在，想留訊息又該如何告知對方呢？讓我們一起來學習這些簡單的電話用語吧！

Telephone Phrases

1 Make a phone call 打電話

Answer by the one you're calling 本人接聽	
Caller	Answerer
Q：I'd like to speak to Ms. Tips, please? 請問題卜老師在嗎？	A：May I ask who's calling, please? 請問你是誰？
^	A：Who is calling/speaking? 請問你哪位？
^	A：May I have your name, please? 請問你的名字是？
^	A：Speaking. 我就是。
Q：Is Ms. Tips there? My name is Ponyo. 請問題卜老師在嗎？我是波妞。	A：Hi, Ponyo. This is Ms. Tips speaking. What's new/up? 嗨，波妞。我是題卜老師。什麼事？

Connecting the one you're calling 請本人來接電話	
Caller	Answerer
Q：Is Ms. Tips in? 題卜老師在嗎？	A：Could you hold on a moment Please? I'll get her. 稍等一下好嗎？我去叫她。
^	A：I'll put her on. 我現在就請她過來接電話。

Transfer the phone call 轉接電話	
Caller	Answerer
Q：Could you put me through to Ms. Tips? 你可以幫我轉接到題卜老師那裡嗎？	A：Just a moment. I will put you through. 請稍等（別掛斷）。我將為你轉接。
^	A：Sure. Could you hold the line? I'll transfer your call to Ms. Tips. 好的。不要掛斷。我將你的電話轉接給題卜老師。
^	A：Certainly. I'll connect you to extension 231. 好的。我幫您轉接到分機 231。

Transfer the phone call 轉接電話

Caller	Answerer
Q：Could you connect me to ext. 231? This is Ponyo calling. I would like to speak to Ms. Tips. 你可以幫我轉接到分機 231 嗎？我是波妞。我想找題卜老師	A：Sorry, Ponyo. She is on another line. 抱歉，波妞。她正在接別的電話。
	A：Sorry, Ponyo. I can't get through to her. The line is busy. 抱歉。波妞。我無法轉分機給她。電話忙線中。
Q：How may I direct your call? 請問要將你的電話轉到哪裡？	A：I'd like to speak to Ms. Tips, please. 我想要跟題卜老師講話，麻煩你轉接。

Make a phone call later 稍後再打

Caller	Answerer
Q：I I'm afraid Ms. Tips is not available at the moment. Do you want to leave a message? 恐怕題卜老師目前無法接聽電話。你想要留訊息嗎？	A：Never mind. I'll call（her）later. 沒關係。我晚一點再打（給她）。

Taking messages 留訊息

Caller	Answerer
Q：This is Ponyo. May I speak to Ms. Tips? 我是波妞。請問題卜老師在嗎？	A：She is not in now. May I take a message? 她現在不在。我可以幫你留訊息嗎？

Request a callback 要求回電

Caller	Answerer
Q：Ms. Tips is out at the moment. Do you want to leave a message? 題卜老師目前外出。你要留訊息給她嗎？	A：Yes. Please tell her to call me back as soon as possible. 好的。請告訴她盡快回電話給我。
	A：Yes, Please tell him Ponyo called. 請告訴她波妞打電話來過。

Unit 11 Make a phone call | 117

Dial a wrong number 打錯電話	
Caller	Answerer
Q：Hello. May I speak to Ms. Tips? 哈囉。請問題卜老師在嗎？	A：I'm afraid you have the wrong number. 恐怕你打錯了。
^	A：There's no one here by that name. 這裡沒有那個人。
^	A：You have the wrong number. 你打錯電話了。
^	A：I'm sorry. I dialed the wrong number. 對不起，我打錯號碼了。

2 Related terms 相關用語

Knock on the door 敲門	
Q：Who is that? 請問你是誰？	A：It's me. Ms. Tips. 是我。題卜老師。

學習完電話相關用語之後，請試著寫寫看吧！

How to answer the question

Conversation 1 : This is Ms. Tips speaking.

Ponyo: May I speak to Ms. Tips?

Ms. Tips: Yes. This is Ms. Tips speaking. May I have your name, please?

Ponyo: This is Ponyo.

Ms. Tips: Hi, Ponyo. What's up?

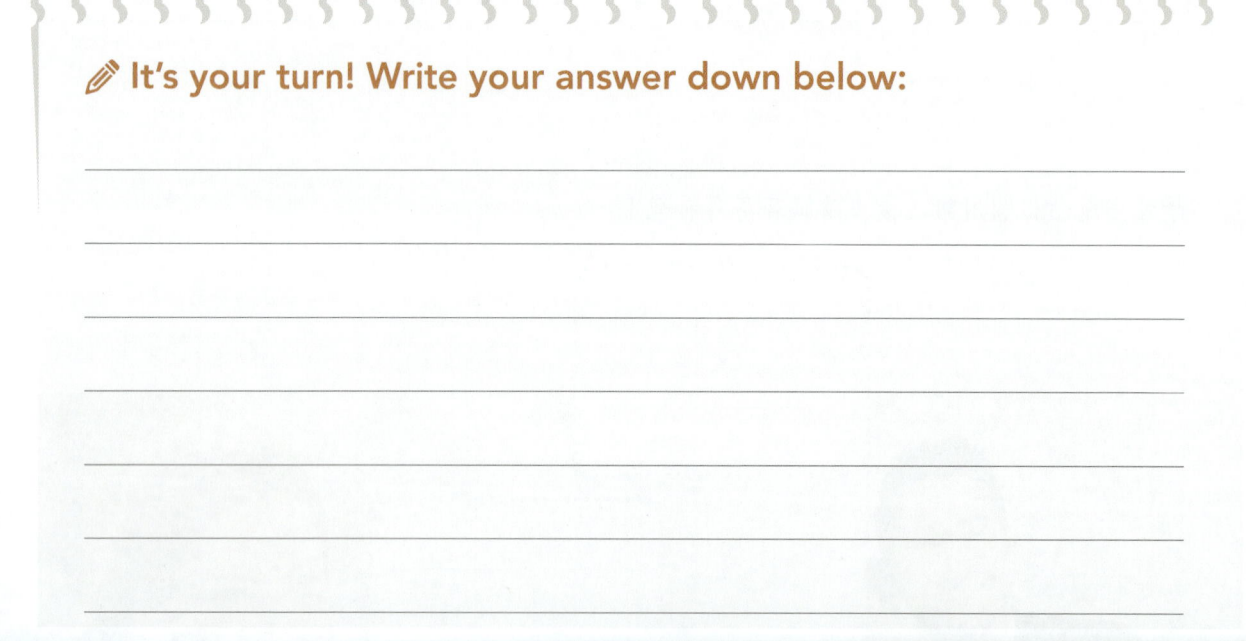

✏️ **It's your turn! Write your answer down below:**

_____
_____
_____
_____
_____
_____

Conversation 2 : I will put her on.

Ponyo: Hi, this is Ponyo. I'd like to speak to Ms. Tips.

Mr. Lin: Hello, Ponyo. Can you hold on a moment? I will put her on.

Ponyo: Thank you.

✏️ **It's your turn! Write your answer down below:**

___
___
___
___
___
___
___

Conversation 3 : I'll transfer your call to Ms. Tips.

Ponyo: Could you please put me through to Ms. Tips? This is Ponyo.

Mr. Lin: Hi, Ponyo. Can you hold the line? I'll transfer your call to Ms. Tips.

Ponyo: Thanks.

Conversation 4 : I can't get through to her. The line is busy.

Ponyo: Could you please connect me to ext. 231? This is Ponyo calling. I would like to speak to Ms. Tips.

Mr. Lin: Hi, Ponyo. Just a moment. I will put you through....Sorry, Ponyo. I can't get through to her. The line is busy.

Ponyo: Never mind. I will call her later.

✏ It's your turn! Write your answer down below:

Conversation 5 : Ms. Tips is out at the moment.

Ponyo: Is Ms. Tips there? This is Ponyo calling.

Mr. Lin: Hi, Ponyo. Ms. Tips is out at the moment. Do you want to leave a message?

Ponyo: Yes. Please tell her to call me back as soon as possible.

✏️ **It's your turn! Write your answer down below:**

I'm afraid you have the wrong number.

Conversation 6 : I'm afraid you have the wrong number.

Ponyo: Is Ms. Tips in? This is Ponyo.

Mr. Wang: I am sorry. There's no one here by that name. I'm afraid you have the wrong number.

✏️ **It's your turn! Write your answer down below:**

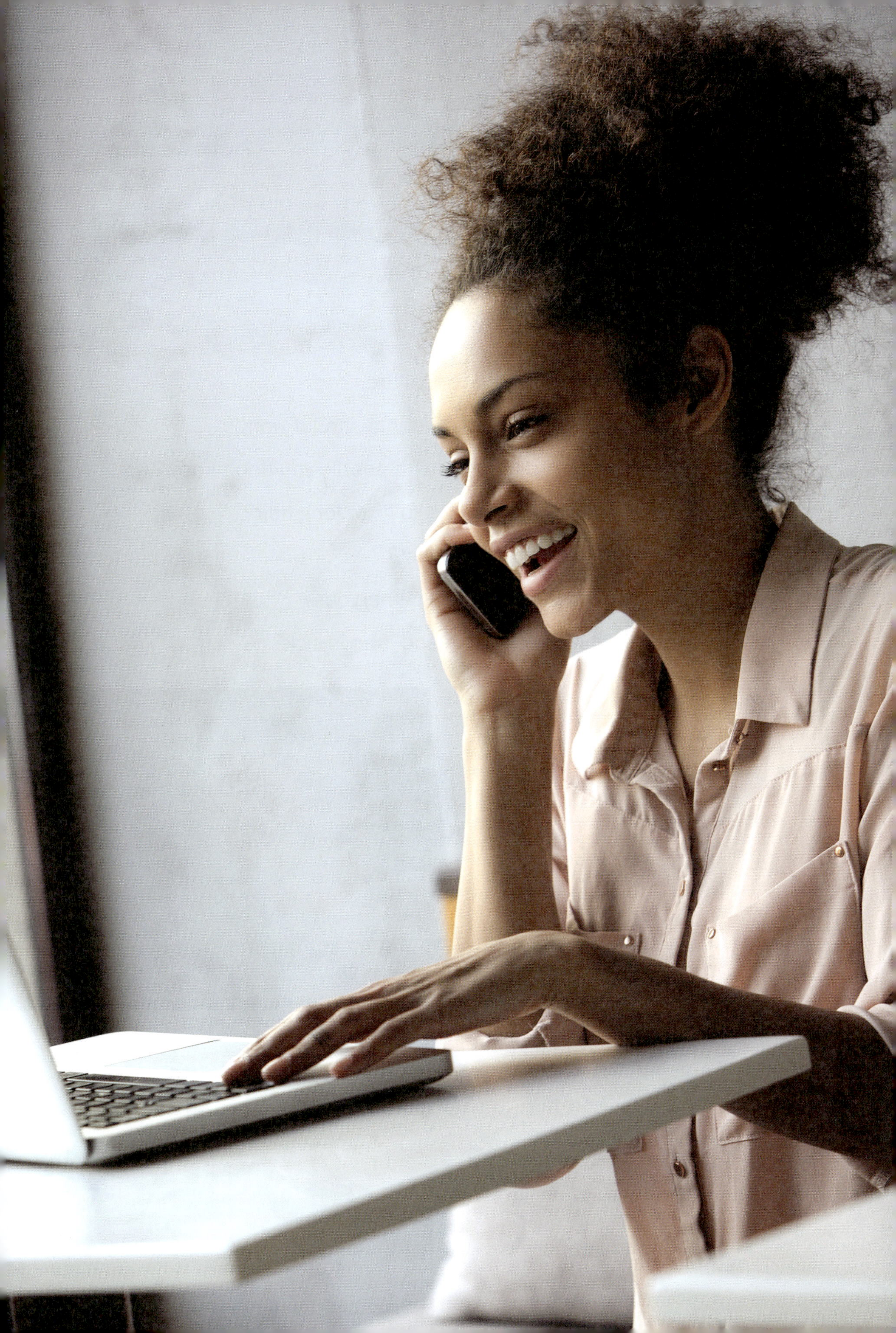

Unit 12

請至 MOSME 觀看教學影片

Opinions and views
描述己見與敘述看法

? Core questions :

Q1. Do you think TV is good for children?

Q2. Do you think high school students should work?

Q3. Do you think it's OK to talk with people you don't know?

Q4. Do you think it's OK for guys to grow long hair?

Q5. How do you feel about this test?

Q6. What kinds of things make you nervous?

Q7. What will you say to your friend if he is sick?

在日常生活中常常需要表達自己對事情的看法與感受，不論是對於看電視或是考試、跟陌生人說話等等。而要如何清楚地描述己見呢？讓我們一起來看看吧！

Ms.Tips & Ponyo's daily conversation

What kinds of things make you nervous?

There are several things that make me nervous.

First, taking exams makes me nervous. I don't do well on schoolwork.

In addition, speaking in front of my class makes me anxious.

What's worse is to see cockroaches. I will scream and run out of the house immediately.

What do you think ?

Phrases to use

1 State your opinion 陳述己見

In my opinion, / From my point of view, / As far as I am concerned,
依我之見

As for me…
至於我

First, / First of all / In the beginning,
首先

In addition, / What's more, / Moreover, / Besides,
首先

Last but not least, / Above all, / The most important is…
最後但同等重要的是最重要的是

What matters is…
要緊的是…

The best thing is…
最棒的是…

What's worse is… / The worst thing is…
更糟糕的是…、最糟糕的是…

2 Emphasizing somthing 強調某事、物

It is 強調的部分 that …

How to answer the question

Q1. Do you think TV is good for children?

Ans.1 Yes. I think TV is good for children. In my opinion, with the advance of science and technology, it is convenient for modern people to have access to a TV, a computer, a cell phone and any other technological devices. TV can provide children with a lot of useful knowledge that they don't learn from school. Therefore, I totally agree that TV is good for children.

Ans.2 Well, from my point of view, I don't think TV is good for children. First of all, some programs on TV are full of violence and bias, which may lead to children's misunderstanding of what happened in the real world. In addition, children may spend more time on TV and less on their schoolwork. Last but not least, watching TV too much may do harm to children's eyesight. Therefore, I think TV is bad for children.

✏️ It's your turn! Write your answer down below:

Q2. Do you think high school students should work?

Ans.1 Yes. I think high school students should work. In my option, there will be three advantages if high school students work. First of all, they can learn what teachers don't teach at school. What's more, they can make friends with people in all walks of work. Last but not least, they can get better understanding about what they can choose as a lifelong career.

Ans.2 No. I don't think high school students should work. As far as I am concerned, there is so much schoolwork that I have to focus on it. I don't have time to take a part-time job. What's more, some working conditions are not safe for high school students to work in. Last but not least, high school students may make friends with bad guys and go astray. In sum, I think that high school students shouldn't work at all.

✏️ **It's your turn! Write your answer down below:**

Q3. Do you think it's OK to talk with people you don't know?

Ans.1 Yes. In my opinion, it is absolutely safe to talk with people I don't know. The strangers may need our help for directions. By the way, I will gain more confidence and courage from the experience of talking to strangers. However, we should stay alert when talking just for our own safety.

Ans.2 No. I don't think it is safe to talk with people I don't know. Since we can't tell good people from bad ones just by appearance, how can we know whether he or she may hurt us or not. Therefore, it is better to keep in a distance with the people I don't know. By the way, it is the way that my mother always teaches me to deal with strangers.

✏️ **It's your turn! Write your answer down below:**

Q4. Do you think it's OK for guys to grow long hair?

Ans.1 Well... From my point of view, it's definitely OK for guys to grow long hair. Everyone in an advanced country has the right to choose what they want to look like, including what to wear and the length of their hair. People should respect each other about that.

Ans.2 I don't agree that guys grow long hair. In my opinion, it is girls that grow long hair. Therefore, it is ridiculous for men and boys to grow long hair. As for me, it will be confusing to tell a man from a woman.

✎ **It's your turn! Write your answer down below:**

Q5. How do you feel about this test?

Ans.1 In my opinion, this test is quite easy. This is the second time I take this test. At the first time, I failed. However, after six months of studying hard, I am confident that I will pass this exam and get the certificate.

Ans.2 Well...my friends said it was easy. As for me, I don't think so. I think it is quite difficult for me. I didn't study hard enough, and I was really nervous when taking this test. It is possible that I will fail this time. I promise that I will study harder from now on.

✏️ **It's your turn! Write your answer down below:**

_____
_____
_____
_____
_____
_____
_____

Q6. What kinds of things make you nervous?

Ans.1 There are several things that make me nervous. First, taking exams makes me nervous. I don't do well on schoolwork. In addition, speaking in front of my class makes me anxious. What's worse is to see cockroaches. I will scream and run out of the house immediately.

Ans.2 Several things make me nervous because I am so shy. First, talking to a stranger makes me nervous. The last time when a stranger came to ask me for directions, I was too nervous to say a word. Besides, when the girl I admire most shows up in front of me, I will be so nervous and act like a fool. Above all, when my teacher asks me to answer the questions in class, I will become dizzy and just stand up there without saying anything. I hope I can be braver in the future.

✏️ **It's your turn! Write your answer down below:**

Q7. What will you say to your friend if he is sick?

Ans.1 If my friend is sick, I will say some things to him. At first, I will ask him to take the medicine. In addition, I will tell him to take care of himself and have more rest. Last but not least, I will give my blessing to him and hope him to recover soon.

Ans.2 There are several things to say to comfort my sick friend. First of all, I will talk to him that he will recover soon to make him feel better. Besides, I will tell him some jokes to make him laugh because smile is the best medicine. At last, I will tell him not to worry about the schoolwork because I will help him with it.

✏️ **It's your turn! Write your answer down below:**

Unit 13

Love or money?
Happy or sad?

二選一

? Core questions :

Q1. Is your family a big one or small one?

Q2. Are you usually happy or sad?

Q3. Do you smile often? Why or why not?

Q4. Is love, or money, more important to you?

Q5. Do you like to sleep late or get up early?

Q6. Would you rather receive letters or e-mails from your friends?

Q7. If you had to live in either Kaohsiung or Taipei, which one would you choose? Why?

請至 MOSME 觀看教學影片

在日常對話中常需要回答二選一的問題，譬如愛情和金錢哪個對你來說更重要？或是你喜歡晚睡或早起？要如何適當地擴充回答，以增加話題呢？一起來看看吧！

GO! GO! GO!

Ms.Tips & Ponyo's daily conversation

Is your family a big one or small one?

My family is a small one.

There are only three people in my family, including my father, my little sister and I.

My father is a laborer and he is kind, honest and hard-working.

My little sister is adorable and has rosy plump cheeks.

> 答句 Tips：二選一的題目，不可用 Yes/No 回答。選項最好從二者之間選一個，並加以說明，或敘述理由。

How to answer the question

Q1. Is your family a big one or small one?

Ans.1 My family is a small one. There are only three people in my family, including my father, my little sister and I. My father is a laborer and my little sister is an elementary school student. My father is kind, honest and hard-working. My little sister is adorable and has rosy plump cheeks*. Though not rich, we lead a peaceful and decent* life.

> 註：只要提到「家人」的題目，都可以參考 U3-Q1。這裡，可以將 U3-Q1 的 Ans.2 應用在此處。

*rosy plump cheeks 紅潤豐滿的臉頰
*decent 體面的

Ans.2 My family is a big one. There are twelve people in my family. They are grandparents, parents, uncle and aunt, three cousins, two brothers and I. We have a big farm, and we grow vegetables and fruit there. We make a living by selling our produce. Though arguing with each other once in a while, we lead a happy and content life together.

> 註：將 U3-Q1 的 Ans.1 加以擴充，應用在此處。

✏️ It's your turn! Write your answer down below:

_____
_____
_____
_____
_____
_____

Q2. Are you usually happy or sad?

Ans.1 I am usually happy. I am an outgoing, energetic and smart girl. I have a lot of activities to do, such as playing badminton, going swimming and playing the piano. I like to make friends with people and I can look at the bright side of things even if some bad things happen. I lead a wonderful life and I am usually happy.

Ans.2 I am usually sad. I am a student now. However, I don't have any interest in schoolwork. What's worse, I am poor at sports. I am too shy to join any sports club and talk with people I don't know. I don't like to go to school at all. Being a student is quite difficult for me.

✏️ **It's your turn! Write your answer down below:**

_____
_____
_____
_____
_____
_____

Q3. Do you smile often? Why or why not?

Ans.1 Yes, I do. I smile often. I am an outgoing, energetic and smart girl. I have a lot of activities to do, such as playing baseball, going shopping and playing mobile games. I like to make friends with people and I can look at the bright side of things even if bad things happen. I lead such a wonderful life that I smile often.

> 註：將上一句 U13-Q2 的 Ans.1 稍微修改，即可應用在此處。

Ans.2 No, I don't smile often and I am usually sad. I am a student now. However, I don't have any interest in schoolwork. What's worse, I am poor at sports. I am too shy to join any sports club and talk with people I don't know. I don't like to go to school at all. Being a student is quite difficult for me.

✏️ **It's your turn! Write your answer down below:**

Q4. Is love, or money, more important to you?

Ans.1 Love, I think. Love is the most wonderful and magic thing in my life. I love my family so much and they love me, too. We share a happy and content life together. We usually go shopping, have a feast and watch TV together. ==In addition==, I love my girlfriend very much. She is brilliant, slender and easy-going. We are movie-goers and we usually have a wonderful time watching movies together. Therefore, I think Love is more important to me.

Ans.2 Well...==In my opinion==, money is more important to me. With money, I can buy a lot of things, go shopping every day, and travel abroad. ==In addition==, I can buy many gifts for my girlfriend, and I can buy an expensive sports car to take her out for a ride. ==What's more==, I can buy a big house for my family to live in. I truly believe the proverb, "==Money talks=="

> 註：講到金錢，有句很簡單的諺語可以背起來喔！
> 「Money talks. 有錢能使鬼推磨。」

✏️ It's your turn! Write your answer down below:

_____
_____
_____
_____
_____

Q5. Do you like to sleep late or get up early?

Ans.1 I prefer to sleep late. As a student, I have to get up early on weekdays. I usually get up at six, or I will miss the school bus at six-thirty. After school, I sometimes have to stay up for the coming exam. Therefore, if I could, I like to sleep late to get enough sleep.

Ans.2 I like to get up early, so I can go jogging in the early morning. When jogging, I can enjoy the fresh air and the wonderful sunrise. After jogging, I go back home to take a shower. I will feel energetic before my daily work begins.

✏️ **It's your turn! Write your answer down below:**

_____
_____
_____
_____
_____
_____
_____

Q6. Would you rather receive letters or e-mails from your friends?

Ans.1 I would rather receive letters. With the advance of technology and science, people seldom write letters. Therefore, if someone writes letter to me, he or she must consider me as an important and special person. That's why I prefer to receive letters rather than e-mails.

Ans.2 I would rather receive e-mails. With the advance of technology and science, it is convenient for modern people to send or receive e-mails. It is faster than letters. By the way, it is easier and cheaper to keep touch with my friends far away by e-mails. Therefore, I prefer to receive e-mails.

✏️ It's your turn! Write your answer down below:

Q7. If you had to live in either Kaohsiung or Taipei, which one would you choose? Why?

Ans.1 As far as I am concerned, I would choose Taipei. Taipei is the biggest city in Taiwan and is famous for its convenient public transportation. People can take the MRT or buses to go to school or work. Therefore, I would like to live in Taipei.

> 註：可以將 U2-Q2 的 Ans.2 應用在此處。

Ans.2 I would choose Kaohsiung. There are several reasons for it. First of all, it is a port city with beautiful views of the ocean. What's more, it is located in southern Taiwan and the weather there is warmer. I prefer sunny days because I can do a lot of outdoor activities, such as going jogging, going picnicking and going hiking. The most important reason is that the living expenses there are much lower than those in Taipei. That helps me save money. That's why I prefer Kaohsiung.

✏️ **It's your turn! Write your answer down below:**

_____
_____
_____
_____
_____
_____

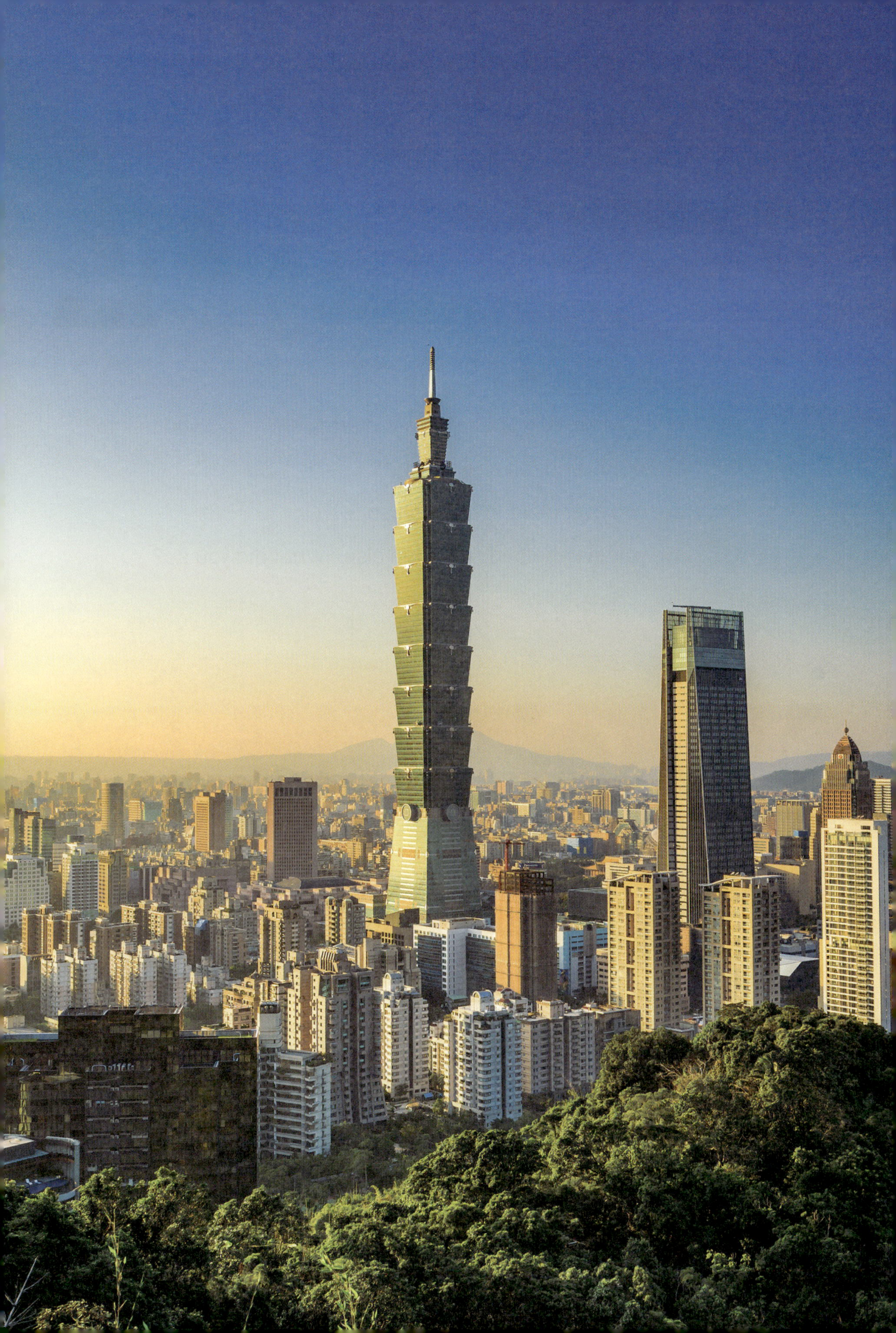

Unit 14

請至 MOSME 觀看教學影片

Past experience
過去經驗

? Core questions :

Q1. Do you ever feel bored?

Q2. Did you make any phone calls yesterday? Who did you talk to?

Q3. Have you ever been to a concert?

Q4. Have you ever slept in class? If so, why?

Q5. Have you ever helped someone else? What did you do?

你曾經在課堂上睡著過嗎?曾經去過演唱會嗎?還是曾經幫助過別人呢?找話題最佳的方法就是詢問別人的過去經驗,一起來看看怎麼說吧!

Let's go!

Ms.Tips & Ponyo's daily conversation

Do you ever feel bored?

Yes, I sometimes feel bored…

When I feel bored, I usually watch TV at home,…

…read fashion magazines in the library or…

…listen to English songs.

We will we will Rock you!

答句 Tips：此章節陳述過去經驗，可以直接將前幾章的回答拿來稍微修改應用。

How to answer the question

Q1. Do you ever feel bored?

Ans.1 Yes, I sometimes feel bored. When I feel bored, I usually watch TV at home, read fashion magazines in the library or listen to English songs. When watching TV, soap opera is my favorite program. It is interesting and exciting. Reading fashion magazines can help me catch up with the modern trend* and fashion. Listening to English songs helps me get rid of the pressure from daily life. *trend 趨勢

Ans.2 No, I never feel bored. I spend a lot of time studying my schoolwork. When I have leisure time, I usually play computer games, read English novels and work out in a gym. Playing computer games is interesting and exciting. Reading English novels can promote my English abilities. Working out in a gym helps me keep in shape. Therefore, I don't feel bored at all.

> 註：若否定回答，也就是從不覺得無聊，即可將 U8-Q3 的 Ans.1 應用在此處。

✏️ **It's your turn! Write your answer down below:**

Q2. Did you make any phone calls yesterday? Who did you talk to?

註：注意答句的時態為「過去式」。

Ans.1 Yes, I made several phone calls yesterday. First, I called my sister to ask her to buy a loaf of bread for me. Then, I called my neighbor to ask him to stop making loud noise because I had to prepare for the coming exam. At last, I made phone calls to my classmates to ask them about some questions in my math and English homework.

Ans.2 No, I didn't make any phone calls yesterday. There were a lot of things I do every day. I am a student now. Yesterday, I went to school in the day time . After school, I did my homework at home. After dinner, I went to a gym to do some weight training to promote my body and health. I didn't call anyone yesterday.

註：若否定回答，接下來可以繼續說昨天做了哪些事。U8 的答句都可以應用在這一題。在此可將 U8-Q5 的 Ans.1 改成過去式，應用在此處。

It's your turn! Write your answer down below:

Q3. **Have you ever been** to a concert?

> 註：注意答句的時態為「現在完成式」。

Ans.1 Yes, I have. I have been to concerts for several times. I like to go to concerts to listen to popular songs and watch my idols' performance. They are exciting, wonderful and help me get rid of the pressure from daily trifles. By the way, My father and my sister enjoy concerts a lot. My father likes to listen to classical music and my sister loves pop music. No matter when and where they go to a concert, I go with them. We usually have a good time together.

> 註：Have you…? 簡答
> Yes, I have.(O)
> Yes, I do/did.(X)

Ans.2 No, I have never been to a concert. I am a student and I have to go to school on weekdays. After school, I usually go to a cram school for further study. When I get home, it is around ten o'clock. Then, I review the lessons and do my homework. When I go to bed, it is nearly midnight. On weekends, I go to a gym to do some weight training to promote my body and health. Therefore, I don't have any spare time to go to a concert.

✏️ **It's your turn! Write your answer down below:**

Q4. Have you ever slept in class? If so, why?

Ans.1 Yes, I have slept in class especially in math classes. Math is my worst subject and math classes are boring to me. I can't calculate well and math is like Greek to me. **By the way**, my math teacher is so strict that many of my classmates are afraid of him.

Ans.2 No, I have never slept in class. As a senior in a senior high school, I have to concentrate on my studies in order to pass the Joint College Entrance Exam. I want to apply for a National University next year, so I study hard and focus on what teachers teach in classes. **By the way**, my teachers are enthusiastic, helpful and humorous. I enjoy Chinese, Math and English classes in particular.

✏ It's your turn! Write your answer down below:

Q5. Have you ever helped someone else? What did you do?

Ans.1 Yes, I have. I have helped others in several ways. **First of all**, I am good at math, so I have helped my classmates with math homework. **In addition**, I can speak English well, and I have guided some foreigners to find the places where they want to go. **Besides**, I have helped my neighbors to look after their babies and pet dogs when they are away. I am glad to help others, because **it is better to give than to receive**.

> 註：It is better to give than to receive.
> 「施比受更有福。」請將此句諺語背起來。

Ans.2 No, I haven't. I don't know how to help others, especially strangers. My mom once told me to watch out for strangers because they might cheat me into buying something or giving them money. **By the way**, I am so shy that I hardly speak anything in front of someone else. Therefore, it is difficult for me to give someone else a hand.

✏️ **It's your turn! Write your answer down below:**

Unit 15

What will you do in these situations?

在…的狀況下，你會怎麼做？

請至 MOSME 觀看教學影片

Core questions:

Q1. If you had one wish, what would it be?
Q2. If your best friend were cheating on a test, what would you do?
Q3. If you found a suitcase with 1,000,000 dollars inside, what would you do?
Q4. If you see someone rob a bank, what would you do?
Q5. What will you do if you have a fever?
What do you usually do when you get a cold?
Q6. What would you change about your school if you could?

在路上如果撿到錢包，裡面有巨額的款項，或是看到有人在搶銀行，你會怎麼辦？生活中常會遇到許多突發狀況，而在這些情況下你會怎麼做呢？來一起看看這類的問題要如何回答吧！

Let's get started!

Unit 15 What will you do in these situations?

Ms.Tips & Ponyo's daily conversation

If you had one wish, what would it be?

I would like to become a beautiful, graceful and smart fairy.

I would be so smart that I could pass all the tests and get good grades.

I could turn bad guys into good ones and make our society a better one.

How to answer the question

Q1. If you had one wish, what would it be?

Ans.1 If I had one wish, I would like to become a beautiful, graceful and smart fairy. I would be so smart that I could pass all the tests and get good grades. By the way, I would be so smart and brilliant that everyone around me likes me. In addition, I could turn bad guys into good ones and make our society a better one.

> 註：形容人「個性」的形容詞請參考U3 +「By the way」、「In addition」。

Ans.2 If I had one wish, I would like to become rich. In my opinion, money is the most important thing to me. With money, I can buy a lot of things, go shopping every day, and travel abroad. In addition, I can buy many gifts for my girlfriend, and I can buy an expensive sports car to take her out for a ride. What's more, I can buy a big house for my family to live in. I truly believe the proverb, "Money talks."

> 註：可以把 U13-Q4 的答句應用在這裡。

✏️ **It's your turn! Write your answer down below:**

_____
_____
_____
_____
_____
_____

Q2. If your best friend were cheating on a test, what would you do?

Ans.1 I would report to my teacher immediately. In my opinion, it is wrong to cheat on the test, even the one cheating on the test is my best friend. I would feel so disappointed about him or her. However, if he can turn over a new leaf, I will forgive him and continue our friendship.

> 註：應用「In my opinion」。

Ans.2 Well. People make mistakes once in a while. A proverb goes "To err is human." In my opinion, if my best friend were cheating on a test, I would do nothing at first. However, after the test, I would warn him or her not to do it again because it is unfair not only to me but also to other students.

> 註：應用「In my opinion」與「佳句 / 諺語」。

✏️ **It's your turn! Write your answer down below:**

_____
_____
_____
_____
_____
_____
_____

Q3. If you found a suitcase with 1,000,000 dollars inside, what would you do?

Ans.1 I would report to my teacher immediately. My teacher is a wise, kind and passionate woman and she always knows what to do. I can always count on her and ask for her advice.

> 註：形容人個性的形容詞，請參考 Unit3。

Ans.2 Well. If I found a suitcase with 1,000,000 dollars inside, I would call the police immediately and ask the police to come over. Before the police come, I would stay with the suitcase to keep it safe. Someone must have forgotten the suitcase and left it there. He or she must be so nervous and upset about having losing the money.

> 註：把問句再重複敘述一次以爭取思考時間。

✎ It's your turn! Write your answer down below:

Q4. If you see someone rob a bank, what would you do?

Ans.1 I would call the police immediately. The police can help people with a lot of difficulties, such as protecting good people from harm and putting bad guys into the prison. In addition, I will stay away from the bank. The robber may carry guns or other weapons, so it is not safe to stay near the bank. By the way, I would call my family and friends just in order to inform them of the news.

> 註：應用 U3-Q6 的 Ans.2 +「In addition」、「By the way」。

Ans.2 If I see someone rob a bank, I would call 110 immediately. In addition, I would turn on my cell phone to record what is happening. By posting the live news on the Internet, I could inform many people of keeping distance from the bank.

✏ It's your turn! Write your answer down below:

_____
_____
_____
_____
_____
_____
_____

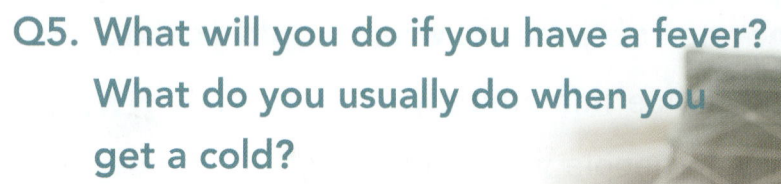

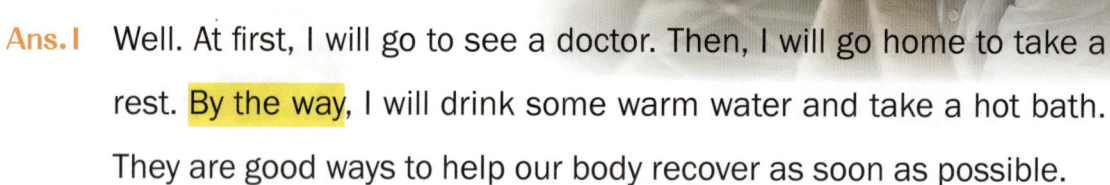

Q5. What will you do if you have a fever? What do you usually do when you get a cold?

Ans.1 Well. At first, I will go to see a doctor. Then, I will go home to take a rest. **By the way**, I will drink some warm water and take a hot bath. They are good ways to help our body recover as soon as possible.

Ans.2 When I get a cold, I won't go to school or work. I will stay at home to take a rest. **In addition**, I will listen to music to relax myself. However, if I get a really bad cold, I will go to see a doctor and take some medicine.

✏️ **It's your turn! Write your answer down below:**

Q6. What would you change about your school if you could?

Ans.1 I would ask to have more PE classes on class schedule. I like to play badminton, baseball and to go swimming in PE classes. Doing exercise can help me keep in shape. By the way, my PE teacher is easy-going, generous and energetic. He teaches me how to play and swim well and helps me to develop good sportsmanship. I have a good time in PE classes.

> 註：應用 U9-Q1 的 Ans.2 +「By the way」。

Ans.2 If I could change something about my school, I would stop any tests or exams at school As far as I am concerned, I have to endure a lot of pressure from taking exams and doing homework. If there were no tests and homework for students, they would become happier and healthier.

✏ It's your turn! Write your answer down below:

書　　　名	高中英文會話素養Easy Go！
書　　　號	PB03401
版　　　次	2019年6月初版 2025年4月二版
編 著 者	許雅惠
責 任 編 輯	楊清淵
校 對 次 數	6次
版 面 構 成	陳依婷
封 面 設 計	陳依婷

國家圖書館出版品預行編目資料

高中英文會話素養Easy Go! / 許雅惠編著. -- 二版. -- 新北市：台科大圖書股份有限公司, 2025.04

面；　公分

ISBN 978-626-391-473-5(平裝)

1.CST:英語　2.CST:會話

805.188　　　　　　　114004787

出 版 者	台科大圖書股份有限公司
門 市 地 址	24257新北市新莊區中正路649-8號8樓
電　　　話	02-2908-0313
傳　　　真	02-2908-0112
網　　　址	tkdbook.jyic.net
電 子 郵 件	service@jyic.net
版 權 宣 告	**有著作權　侵害必究** 本書受著作權法保護。未經本公司事前書面授權，不得以任何方式（包括儲存於資料庫或任何存取系統內）作全部或局部之翻印、仿製或轉載。 書內圖片、資料的來源已盡查明之責，若有疏漏致著作權遭侵犯，我們在此致歉，並請有關人士致函本公司，我們將作出適當的修訂和安排。
郵 購 帳 號	19133960
戶　　　名	台科大圖書股份有限公司 ※郵撥訂購未滿1500元者，請付郵資，本島地區100元 / 外島地區200元
客 服 專 線	0800-000-599
網 路 購 書	勁園科教旗艦店　蝦皮商城　　博客來網路書店　台科大圖書專區　　勁園商城
各服務中心	總　　公　　司　02-2908-5945　　台中服務中心　04-2263-5882 台北服務中心　02-2908-5945　　高雄服務中心　07-555-7947 線上讀者回函 歡迎給予鼓勵及建議 tkdbook.jyic.net/PB03401